The Wrong Sister . . .

The moonlight on the castle battlements was lovely. And I knew it was moon-madness, but it was literally impossible to pretend coyness, to reject Rupert, when every nerve in my body tingled. If this was all I'd ever know of love, these moments were still worth it.

I was clinging to him, kissing him back—when suddenly he thrust me away with a groan. "Enough of this imposture," he said harshly. *"Du bist nicht Nyx, du bist Katie."*

You are not Nyx, you are Katie.

He knew! He flung away, burying his head against his arms, while I sank into the nearest seat, totally stunned. And my heart sank too. Not only was my love hopeless—but how would I rescue my sister now? . . .

A LANCER ORIGINAL

DARK MOON, LOST LADY

ELSIE LEE

LANCER BOOKS • NEW YORK

A LANCER BOOK • 1965

DARK MOON, LOST LADY

LANCER BOOKS, INC. • 185 MADISON AVE. • NEW YORK, N.Y. 10016

Chapter I

THE ENVELOPE had been forwarded from San Sebastian to Madrid to Naples, but when I ripped it open with a sigh of relief, it contained only a postcard. It was one of the small European snobberies: a glossy photograph of the family residence, printed in three languages, ready for guests to mail to friends back home. This particular family residence was a breath-taking castle, complete with battlements and towers, looking as though it sprang full-panoplied from the impregnable rock crags upon which it sat. The photographer had caught a wide angle, apparently in spring, so that flowering sprays formed a natural frame through which one saw the castle entire, as well as the huge headland outthrust into the shimmering waters of the Rhine.

Wow, was that where my sister and I were going to spend the summer! I had no need to read the fine print; I knew the place, even though I hadn't seen this view before. It was Stelleberg, property of Prince Rupert von Aspern, and Magneciné had rented it as a setting for a modern fairy-tale film that was going to be very artistic, with my sister as the star.

I turned the card over and gasped involuntarily. In very flowing ink, the message read: "Having wonderful time, wish you were here." There was no signature, but I needed none—and all the vague uneasiness of the past ten days was back. I fished the envelope from the trash basket. It was hard to separate postmarks, and sheer luck I'd never gotten it, but the original stamp was German, the Madrid date only three days past. Working backward, I knew the envelope must originally have been mailed about ten days ago —or exactly when I'd first known something was wrong.

At the time, the friends with whom I had been about to tour Calabria concealed well-bred surprise at my vehement refusal to leave Reggio until I made phone calls. If there is anything more maddening than European phone service, I don't know it—but eventually I got a whistly voice that said, *"Die Fraulein vorn das schloss heraus ist."* Then the operator somehow cut us off, and I never did get Stelleberg again. An hour later I reached Flip Hogarth at the Magnaciné office in Rome.

At least, he didn't need explanations. When I said, "I have a *feeling*," he was serious at once. "I had a letter from her this morning, Katie, and if they said she was *out*, it couldn't be anything dire. Your ESP reaches deep, you know."

I had to agree, and when he swore by the hairs in his mother's mustache he'd keep calling Stelleberg every fifteen minutes day and night, I laughed helplessly and rang off. No question he'd do it more easily from Cinecitta than I could in Calabria, but I was still vaguely troubled for a few days. Then the feeling went away. I decided Flip was right about ESP, because it does reach deep between my sister and me. For example I once roused everyone at dead of night, insisting there'd been a disaster. It later developed she'd merely burnt her tongue on a cup of hot bouillon, while sitting up late to read a script.

So from Reggio, we drove to Catanzara and on through innumerable villages around the Gulf until we came to Taranto, debating a side trip to Bari before striking up to Potenza and back to Naples. Now, holding the card in trembling fingers, I was devoutly thankful we'd been surfeited with motoring, hence in Naples several days earlier than planned.

I left the luggage as it was, and requested a call to Flip, *Subito, es una emergencia!* I studied the card again, eyes closed and concentrating—and quite apart from the message which was our private code, I *felt* shock, fright, amounting to terror. It was only in the card; when I picked up the envelope, I felt nothing.

Strange . . .

I lit a cigarette, forced myself to calm consideration, but there was still nothing. Or was there? Our physicist father has an axiom: No result is still a valuable end product; knowing what does not work eliminates waste time.

My sister had never handled this envelope. That was why I got nothing from it. I took it to the light and scrutinized the original address. It was half-obscured by the forwardings, but although the general flowing style had been duplicated, even to the same broad-nib pen, I knew at once. I might have known even before I opened it, except for being so relieved to have word.

Superficially, it passed muster because I was concerned with the *contents*, but whoever had mailed the card had made one tiny mistake. The direction was to Miss Katherine Hume, and in itself that told me the writer was German, trapped by the usual Teutonic spelling.

On my birth and baptismal certificates, my name is spelt "Catherine." I am called Katie—to distinguish me from my Aunt Cathy, who is still the right side of fifty and married to a millionaire oil bigwig. This is why I had a deluxe education and possess a modest private income. It's that simple, and my sister has never cavilled at the fact she was named for Aunt Margaret, whose husband did not turn out to be a modern robber baron.

"I've already made all the money I'll ever need, in spite of taxes, darling—and I *like acting*," she had said. "I'll probably go on as long as anyone'll hire me, while you never really latched onto anything you yearned to work at—so why shouldn't you be endowed for independence, and fiddle about, taking care of me for as long as you like? A very comfortable arrangement, I calls it!"

It was, on the whole. Our mutual ESP was often more irritating than helpful. But ever since I had a nasty ski accident, and someone had distractedly mailed the postcard I hadn't finished, so that it arrived without signature . . . and taking it from the postman, my sister had *known* I was in trouble—those trite words meant: *à moi, à l'instant!*

We hadn't used the message often, as we are not the sort of girls who get into serious predicaments. Once, when she was innocently involved in an auto accident, and the local bureaucratic red tape needed cutting—once, when someone officiously stuck me in a hospital and the doctor was all for padding his fee . . . This was Europe, not America, however—not a matter of home ground; I had to plan carefully, go slow or perhaps make things worse.

Rome, first, of course. Flip would know lawyers, doctors, how to deal with Europeans . . . part of his job was to know how to extricate Hollywood stars from difficulties, although he'd never had to worry about my sister before.

There was a single seat on the Roma plane, leaving in forty-five minutes. "I'll take it, send for my luggage, prepare the bill, have a car waiting," I said, "and keep trying on that phone call to Rome, you understand?"

"*Si*, but—la Signorina abandons her room?"

"*Doni al nonimpiego.*" I hung up on his shocked gasp at the mere idea of a hobo occupying one of the best beds, and got ready to travel: fresh make-up, wash the hands, check passport and money. The Challoners were more difficult. "So sorry, something's come up and I must leave at once, an emergency—but you do understand?"

"No, I can't say I do," Ian Challoner began in a

nonsense British voice, while Moira bleated, "Where are you going? Is this wise, Katie? We've only just arrived . . ."

"To Rome, and it's not only wise but essential." I shook hands heartily, "Keep in touch, please? 'Byeee . . ." I left them standing at their door, peering blankly at a bellboy whapping my bags on a carrier and strutting away to the elevator.

From force of habit, I took a final glance about my room, though I'd unpacked nothing—but there was still the card and the envelope. Hastily I stuffed them into my handbag together with a packet of matches, and fled down the hall. By experience, I trotted down the stairs—and the bill was paid, the call cancelled ("There is still no circuit, *dolersi di ditti*") just as the boy panted from the elevator to hurl my bags into the cab.

Smiles, bows, rushings about, and largesse . . . twenty minutes later I sat in the plane for Rome, with an hour to consider where do we go from here? Instinct said "Germany"; caution said, "Don't addle the eggs!"

All I knew was that my sister had met Prince Rupert von Aspern, seen pictures of Schloss Stelleberg, and instantly decided it was *right* for her film. By the time I reached Cannes and met her, the deal had been made and His Highness had returned to Germany . . . but from the tone of her voice, I suspected *love* had caught up with her. She was open as always with details of parties and excursions, who was there, what she wore—but I noticed his name figured prominently in every story.

There seemed not to be any letters or phone calls from Germany, but I was unsurprised when there was a formal invitation for her to stay a month before the filming was to begin . . . spidery violet ink on thin crested notepaper, signed Adelheid, P.

It was all very correct, very *comme il faut*, and fooled no one, least of all Flip Hogarth who had been madly in love with my sister from the moment Magneciné had first signed her, ten years before. He came up from Rome, ostensibly to consult about script changes, but his spaniel eyes looked beaten when the Wiesbaden plane took off.

"I'm sorry, Flip, but it may not come to anything," I told him.

He did not pretend to misunderstand. "Don't count on it, Katie. It's the first time in all these years—and he's genuine: title, enough money, and the family were never Nazi. Don't think I didn't check!" Flip said grimly. "Well, they were high on the Nazi proscribed list. They nipped across the Rhine one night, with all the valuables—tucked the old lady in Switzerland, and turned up next day, asking to join an army—any army.

"There was Rupert and three younger brothers. They ended in the underground: The middle boys were killed when someone informed a Maquis operation—pure luck Rupert wasn't with it—and the kid Kaspar was so young he only ran errands." Flip shrugged. "CIA, OSS, British Intelligence—everyone gives him a clean slate. He's put the castle in running order; he's on every planning commission for revitalizing Germany, Bonn depends on him, he makes unofficial suggestions to our people in Frankfort and Wiesbaden, never known to be wrong, pulls them out of potential boo-boos.

"He's forty years old, unmarried, and not bad-looking," Flip sounded discouraged. "I guess I've had it, Katie."

I felt a bit discouraged, myself. I'd always liked the idea of Flip for a brother-in-law. "It may not come to anything," I repeated hopefully. "She's never much cared for foreigners or titles, you know."

Flip was not cheered. "Yes—but he's got everything to go with it."

Bucketing about in the Rome plane, I tried to plan constructively. Perhaps this prince *was* the right man —although in that case, how could he have allowed my sister to be terrified? Still, it might have been temporary; after all, I'd lost my *feeling* in a few days and only regained it with the arrival of the card. The card merely confirmed that something *had been* wrong . . . it might, by now, be entirely smoothed out. In which case, how would she explain a wild-eyed sister bursting in, babbling "What *happened?*" It could easily queer the romance—and romance is basic in our family.

I expect that has to be explained, because there is no doubt that we're peculiar. Our friends call us "gifted"; other people think we are mad. The fact remains that we all possess extraordinary ESP—but only for special people. Mother is artistic; Daddy is the sort of physicist who periodically vanishes and cannot talk about his work. In between, he holds seminars for physics grad students with an IQ of 150 or better. Mother says he will win a Nobel Prize this year, and as she knew (and had ordered a gown) even before Daddy had time to wire about dinner at the White House before a Congressional award, we assume she is right.

The same unspoken communication between our parents exists between my sister and me, although they have become calmer. Daddy no longer bolts a Washington conference to phone whenever mother has sliced her finger with a fruit knife in California, so we hope we will eventually get the hang of it.

I am less than a year older than my sister. Georgie and Sylvia are spaced respectably, post-war and three years apart. They are companionable, but have only occasional flashes of telepathy. We do not know whether it is the difference in age, or the difference in sex. However, neither of them will ever play bridge against any combination of the rest of us.

So my sister and I are not twins, but if one sees us separately, it's hard to tell which is who. Side by side, it's easy, because she is *more* everything. We both have masses of long silky black hair; hers is longer and thicker. We both have deep-set hawks' eyes, hers are *blue*-blue, mine are faintly greenish. She is an inch taller, an inch smaller at the waist, subtly finer boned. We have the same thin straight noses, faintly pointed chins and the Hume dimple to the left of our mouths. Most of all, we have the same translucent skin.

For a party gag, my sister borrows a pencil flashlight and sticks it in her mouth after the lights are turned out. The result looks like a match within an old Limoges cup. I look the same way, but it is her trick and I never use it—because we divided everything between us when we were thirteen. I took the double-joined thumb; we thought it wouldn't be nearly so useful for an actress—and my sister was always going to be an actress.

"But why? You can't possibly want to be like those creatures at Malibu—hair all shrivelled from dye, skin all puckered from make-ups . . ."

"No, of course not, Katie. I shall be different."

When I was fourteen, Aunt Cathy sent me to Miss Porter's, then on to Radcliffe, with two months of each summer spent in Europe. My sister went to school in Beverly Hills, where she had the dubious distinction of being the only student who ever made bottom of the class in every subject for four years straight. With one exception: English, at which she was A Honors. Her successive Class Day performances as Puck, Miranda, Kate and Desdemona got her a diploma. Faced with the depressing concept of limitless years in which Margaret Hume would become an aging Sixth Former, the teaching staff spoke to Miss Spencer—who sent for Daddy.

"I will sign this diploma only if you guarantee *not* to send Margaret to college, Professor Hume."

"*College?*" said Daddy, honestly startled. "Good heavens, *no!* She's totally uneducable, hasn't the wits of a flea. *I* understood Meg wanted to be an actress, it's all she's good for."

"Yes, but I expect she'll be very good at that," Miss Spencer murmured, signing the diploma.

And she was.

While I was coping with Economics and Philosophy at Radcliffe, Meg simply walked into the anteroom of Magneciné and said, "My name is Margaret Hume, and I've come to act for you." There was more to it, of course, but eventually she was cast for side roles in remakes of Edgar Allen Poe or juvenile surfing epics. By the time I graduated and was wondering, "Now what?", Meg had equally graduated from her apprenticeship, with a cagy escalator contract—and a new name.

"Nyx," she said, widening her eyes at me. "Greek, I think."

"Yes, Nyx is the goddess of night," I looked at her analytically. "A good name for you."

"What are you going to do, Katie—I mean, when you get back from Spain?"

"I don't know, I hadn't thought about it."

"You could always stand in for me. I can have one, now. Why not? *Why not, Katie?*" We looked at ourselves, standing side by side mirrored in the bathroom door. "If only you could act, we could take turns."

"Well, I can't and I don't want to, but I don't mind giving you a hand now and then."

It worked amazingly well, once people got used to seeing Nyx leave a set while apparently simultaneously entering on the opposite side. We decided to use Meg's professional name all the time, to emphasize star status, and we developed separate mannerisms so people could tell us apart. Actually, it was great fun, building her a public personality.

Nyx naturally acquired specialties from her various roles: a way of walking, using her hands, turning her head. These were her trademarks to film audiences all over the world. Once she'd set something, I learned it at home, so I could take her place in public, if I had to. Then I deliberately adopted something glaringly different for use when we were on set together.

The simplest touch was wearing my hair in a braided coronet and speaking with an Eastern accent, while Nyx deepened her voice for better reproduction. After a while, we were so entirely distinct from each other, aside from facial resemblance, that no one ever realized we *could* still double on demand!

We split the house she bought in the Valley in half; we had private friends, friends in common. Sometimes we were both home, sometimes we were away. The money I made as stand-in, and later as her personal representative, amplified Aunt Cathy's endowment to luxury status. There was a complicated tax set up, whereby we were both incorporated and paid each other for this and that from company funds—or something.

Occasionally, we doubled for each other. It was I who accepted the Oscar—and gallant two-cheek kisses from Sir Laurence Olivier—while Nyx was bundled on the couch, mopping up a cold with a giant-size box of Kleenex. "Didn't you *wish* you were there?"

"Heavens, no—*much* more fun to watch myself. You did it marvelously, darling; that bit with the wrist was awfully effective. D'you mind if I take it?"

"Of course not, I've no particular use for it."

"Are you sure? You aren't losing your identity, are you?"

I was surprised at her troubled voice. "Does it seem so?"

"No, but I mightn't realize." Nyx growned, faintly anxious. "Propinquity, you know. What's ahead for you, Katie? I know where I'm going, and I'm getting there faster with your help, but we must be careful not to sacrifice you for me, darling."

"Marriage, you mean?"

"Yes—or do you like being alone? You've enough money, of course."

"What about you? You've enough money, too."

"Yes. We'd better think about it . . ."

So we *thought*, and agreed marriage might be difficult, but ought to be on the agenda. "If I marry first, it won't matter—unless you don't like him," Nyx said. "It'd just be a man in my part of the house."

"You wouldn't marry anyone I didn't like. I mean you wouldn't be attracted by anyone who wouldn't be attractive to me, too, even if I didn't want to marry him."

"Yes, or you, either. We needn't worry about that."

"No, but if I marry first, I'll leave. I don't think we'd like me to have a husband who was content to live in a wing of his famous sister-in-law's home, no matter how we did it financially."

"The thing is," Nyx said, "I'm still busy; I haven't come to the end of where I know I can go. It might take another ten years, Katie, but unless I find someone exceptional, I don't care. Ye're only twenty-five; I could still have babies in ten years." So we

17

agreed: Marriage for both of us, probably me before Nyx, but even if life was immensely comfortable now, we'd better start looking about seriously.

In three years, neither of us had really found any one she wanted. Now it was possible Nyx thought she had someone—but why should it lead her to shock, terror, an SOS to me . . . then, apparently, a fade-out?

As the landing signs flashed on, I concentrated—and I *knew* Nyx was physically safe, but I suddenly felt anger and determination. Wherever she was, Nyx was seething with fury—not one of the rare, carefully calculated, film-star storms of temperament, but genuine *fury*.

I closed my eyes and said mentally, *Don't worry, I'm coming*. We'd never tried for verbal telepathy, but apparently we could do it. Just as the plane hit the runway with a horrid jolt, I sensed a sort of sigh of relief.

I entrusted my bags to a porter, I went into the Ladies'—and I came out as Nyx.

I ran the gauntlet of the filthy ill-bred rudeness of Rome reporters, ignoring the backside pinches (I'd be livid in two hours; I bruise easily), and graciously signing photographs. That was simple, because the first thing we'd done was standardize our writing of *Nyx* for exactly this sort of crisis. I gave the porter an outrageous tip and hissed, "*Incognito! Non parli!*" and nipped into the taxi, knowing perfectly well he'd pick up large quantities of lire for a minute description of his encounter with Nyx, the glamorous, the famous.

Thirty minutes later I was walking into Flip's office, saying, "Flip darling—how are you?" The blinds were tilted to create dusk against the brilliant late afternoon sun, and I fooled him. It was all I needed to tell me . . .

He slammed down the phone without even saying "Gotta go now." He tore out from behind the desk and caught me in his arms with such strength I nearly screamed, talking-talking between hugs and kiss-cuddlings. "Nyx, baby—what happened, where have you been? Oh, sweetie, if you ever do this again, I'll break your pretty little neck! Why in hell go to Paris, why not tell where you're staying? My God, I even had the Sureté checking hotels . . ."

Paris?

"I suddenly thought, Why not Balenciaga for the ball gowns in Act II? So I dashed up—and I stayed with the Laurents," I said experimentally in Nyx's voice, "but I did let you know . . ."

"A lousy ten-word telegram," he snarled, half-shaking me. "Dammit, Nyx, you went to school—you must be able to write even if you have to print. You could have sent a *card* at least, saying where you were. What 'n hell I'll tell the Sureté!" He let me go with a groan of frustration, clutching his sandy red curls wildly. "Give me a story, baby: *why?*"

I shrugged. "I got *bored*, darling; I excused myself, to consult about costumes—had to say *something*—and of course I can write, but why bother? I never dreamed you'd *worry*, Flip, darling—and actually, I simply didn't want to hear from anyone. Understand?"

"No," he said baldly, thrusting past me to the phone. "Get me Inspector Dubois in Paris—Steinman in Hollywood—Miss Hume at the Castello in Naples," he barked, while I drifted to the window, humming to myself and fiddling with the cord of the blind—the complete picture of an intransigent film star, uninterested in how much difficulty she might cause. Below me, the workers of Cinecitta were streaming toward the front gates, laughing, talking, clapping each other on the back—and behind me, Flip jiggled the phone frantically . . . said, "Cancel all those calls, please," and swept the instrument crashing to the floor, to stand up, leaning on clenched hands that were white at the knuckles and stare at me.

"What're you trying to pull?" he asked harshly. "You're not Nyx—you're Katie . . ."

Chapter II

"Yes," I said, glancing at my wrist watch in a sliver of light through the blinds. For ten full minutes I'd fooled a man who'd been wildly in love with my sister for as many years. "Where is she, Flip?"

"In Paris, according to the telegram." He scrabbled nervously on the desk and threw the flimsy at me, sinking back into his chair with a groan. "My God, Katie, how can you be so cruel?" He buried his face in his hands, while I looked at the message: *Having wonderful time wish you were here Nyx.*

I tossed it atop the untidy desk, went around to lay an arm about his shoulders. "I'm never cruel," I said, as evenly as I could. "Pull yourself together, Flip—because something is really wrong and we have to figure it out."

He drew a long breath, patted my hand briefly. "I need a drink; fix for us, Katie." He jerked a finger toward a bar cart, and collapsed into his chair, white-faced, eyes closed. It was not like Flip to be unstrung merely because he'd been kissing *me* wildly and found he'd got the wrong girl; far more likely he'd demand a retake, on the score he'd never tried me before or was conducting a poll or something. He was well-named; his mind was as Flip as he was.

I brought him scotch on the rocks. "How did you know?"

"You were humming on key," he said dully, tossing down half the liquid at a gulp, while I mentally kicked myself. Such a silly simple thing: to forget Nyx wasn't musical in any way—and I couldn't draw even a crooked line that looked like anything.

"Where is she?" I asked again, fixing my own drink.

"God knows," he said after a moment and finished his glass, springing up to prepare a generous refill. He turned toward me, glass in hand, bracing himself. "*Or you,*" he said, all defenses down. "Is she—dead, Katie? *Tell me true!*"

"No, she's physically safe, but I don't know where, except something has made her very angry." I took a sip of my highball. "And where were *you* when the lights went out? Ten days ago you swore you'd check, while I was in Calabria; two days later the heat in my mind went off. I assumed you'd reached Nyx, that she was all right. Nothing bothered me until I hit Naples today.

"I got a card; she'd written it, Flip. But she hadn't written the envelope in which it was mailed to me ten days ago . . . at which point she was *terrified*. That's gone—but if she was ever in Paris, I'll eat it. She would never send you *that* particular message. It has a special meaning to *us*," I finished evenly. "So—where were you?"

"In New York, but as heaven is my witness, I *thought* she was at Stelleberg when I left. It was only the wire, with no address—and not being able to reach anyone . . ." he muttered. "Oh, they were perfectly polite at Stelleberg—but they only knew she'd left, with no forwarding address."

"Hmmm, yes, I don't wonder you were uneasy. She never vanishes without alerting you. Sit down, Flip, and let's start when we saw her onto the plane at Cannes. I had two letters, which was two more than I expected—you know Nyx and letter writing, but these were *screeds*, ten or more pages, and I'd swear there was nothing wrong then. What about you?"

"I had the usual deluge of scrawled notes," he said, slowly. "Tell Lew, and cable Rosie—*you* know. She called once about the script, and she sounded—happy. And once I phoned her about the mobile dressing rooms."

"*Exactly* the date of your call? Are you sure it was Nyx?"

"Yes." He pulled out his day book, riffling pages. "It was Nyx herself, she told me to buy Pundit a pound of shrimps for his birthday." Pundit is Flip's Siamese cat, who goes wherever Flip goes, and traditionally Nyx provides a feast of shrimps—who but Nyx would know that? "Here it is," he said, "May 15, four p.m."

I studied the wall calendar. "When is Pundit's birthday?"

"May 20th, why?"

"I'm pinpointing. As of the 15th, she was there. Were you conscious of strain or nervousness?"

He shook his head. "Rotten connection, as always, but she bubbled along about a village festival and Sunday on the river. There were names, references—I don't recall, but it was she, and she was perfectly happy."

"But within the next two to three days, she'd been so alarmed that she wrote the card—and then had no chance to send it," I reflected. "They sent it to San Sebastian; Nyx would have mailed it care of you."

"In heaven's name, why?"

"You're our *pivot*," I said, surprised. "Didn't you know? I always tell you where I am; it's your business to know where Nyx is—so if she's not where I think she is, or vice versa, we keep in touch through you, because we always do know where you are, Flip."

"In the middle, behind the eight-ball," he agreed, bitterly.

There was a long silence. "Why? Didn't you ever speak up?"

"How could I? Suppose I'd caught her young, when she was uncertain how things'd go for her? She had to have her chance—it paid off in blue chips, and now . . . how could Nyx marry a mere studio boy?"

"Very easily, I should say—and you're much more than a studio boy, Flip. If anything, you're her Svengali," I remarked. "*You* named her Nyx—and believe me, my sister Margaret was never uncertain how things were to go for a single moment in her life."

Flip took a long breath. "Okay, I'm a coward, afraid to lay it on the line. If she said *no*, I'd lose what I've got—and over the years, it's built into quite a lot. I

24

can be with her, talk to her, nearly every day; it's me she turns to for nearly everything. She—consults me, confides things—sometimes silly details she doesn't even tell you. She asks my opinion, and you'd be astounded how often, when she's thought it over, she'll agree I was right."

He rumpled his hair distractedly, while I stared at him, fascinated by this sidelight on my sister. "It may be only half a loaf, but I've grown to depend upon it. I can't risk losing it, don't you see?"

"What I see is a big fatheaded *jerk!*" I told him crossly. I'd always known he adored Nyx; until this moment, I'd never known how she felt about him— and the mere fact that she'd kept Flip private from me told me he was *it.* I couldn't have been happier—or more furious that he'd diddle-dawdled until she'd decided to needle him with jealousy. I said so, in basic terms. "Flip Hogarth, who d'you think you are— some medieval troubadour, who hasn't guts enough to get a duplicate key for the chastity belt? Abelard or Petrarch—or a stupid Leander shivering in the Hellespont?

"She's done everything but a naked grind and bump in front of you, trying to get you to say 'Will you marry me?'," I snarled, "and you sit there like a clod, bleating, 'I can't lose what I have!' You bloody fool, don't you realize she's already *mentally* married to you?

"As of now, your Milquetoast stupidity has egged Nyx into this Teutonic frou-frou which has obviously landed her in a first class *mess.* So if you want her, you will now be a knight in shining armor, or," I said silkily, "perhaps you prefer status quo? Delicate yearning, the might-have-been, titwillow, titwillow—and a comfortable bachelor existence?"

"No!" Flip sprang up and glared at me. "Dammit, Katie—I was only trying for the right moment, when she'd be ready."

"She's evidently been ready for some time, and so have I. You'll be exactly the brother-in-law to my taste."

"You're not just saying that to make me feel good?"

"What I'm going to say isn't designed to make you feel anything but criminally negligent," I told him grimly. "As of noon, May 18th, I told you something was wrong; you swore you'd keep trying until you got Nyx. I depended on you. Now we've lost ten days."

"I did try. Every time I got the castle, she was asleep, or had gone out; they never said she'd left, just that she couldn't come to the phone. I thought she'd return a call eventually," he said, pulling himself together with an effort. "Then there was a major crisis about public domain and royalties; I had the documents here, but they needed me in New York for depositions. The last time I reached Stelleberg was about six p.m.

"They said Fraulein Hume was in the path, preparing to dress for dinner . . . there's only one phone, you know, down in the library near the porter's office . . ."

"How—convenient," I narrowed my eyes thoughtfully.

"I'd say it's damned inconvenient," he snorted. "Naturally, she couldn't climb out of a tub and paddle downstairs in a robe and slippers! They asked for a message; I said to tell her I had to go to New York and was there anything she'd like me to do stateside. They said to wait; I did, and in a few minutes they said the Fraulein had no commissions, to let her know when I returned.

"My God, Katie, why would I doubt she was *there?*" he said, anguished. "When they kept trotting back and forth with messages . . ."

"What makes you think she provided the answers?" I asked. "What *day* was this, Flip?"

"Wednesday . . ."

"May 20th—Pundit's birthday," I said softly. "You know Nyx, Flip—she'd never have forgotten to ask if you'd bought his shrimps, say 'Kiss him for me'—*not if she remembered him five days earlier*. Wasn't there a message for Pundit, Flip?"

His face was ashen, tortured. Wordlessly, he shook his head. "I was so off my head with all I had to do—they only gave me two hours, Katie," he said finally, "and when the porter was apparently going up and downstairs . . . The last message was 'Fraulein Hume says have fun and telephone when you return'."

"Have fun is a standard; they hit it by chance. It convinced you because you were harassed—but *Nyx wasn't there*," I sighed. "They've a ten-day headstart."

"They?"

"Or he, she, or it," I said impatiently, and went

around the desk to hug him gently. "Flip, hon—I'd like you for a brother; I suspect Nyx wants you for a husband."

"Would you really not mind, Katie? I wouldn't take her away from you, you know."

"Bless you, sweetie, I don't have Nyx any more than she has me," I said, surprised. "You might as well worry whether I'd be in *your* way."

"Of course not!"

"That's why you're ideal for Nyx, because you're used to me. Even today, when I deliberately pretended, I only fooled you for ten minutes, but if you were family, we'd always tell you if we had to double for each other. We never play tricks in the family."

"Double . . . You mean, Nyx pretends to be *you?*" he said, dazedly. "My God, I never knew . . . never dreamed . . ."

"We don't do it often," I soothed, "but if you never guessed, it's certain no one else ever did. It might be our ace in the hole. You will now phone for a suite at the Excelsior for Miss Hume, you will fix me another drink and dig out every note from Nyx, while I visit the lavabo."

"You'll need a key . . ."

We saw it simultaneously, lying in the center of his secretary's desk: this morning's *Le Figaro*, with a news photo of Nyx in the doorway of Lanvin-Castillo. For a moment, we stared in silent shock. Then Flip grabbed the paper in shaking hands.

"Look—she *is* there! Dammit, whoever said foreign secretaries are superior to American should be hung," he raved. "The stupid idiot! She *knows* I'm trying to reach Nyx—yet she finds a picture on the front page of a newspaper, and calmly walks off without telling me . . ."

"Remember your blood pressure," I said absently, twitching the paper away from him and turning on the desk light. "I don't know why the girl didn't tell you—maybe she thought you already knew—but in any case, *look again*. It's a fuzzy shot, but if Nyx is your girl, you know her." I positioned myself roughly to reproduce the photograph—smiling, hand raised graciously. "Well?"

Flip took one comparative glance, and dropped the paper, pulling out a handkerchief to mop his forehead. He sagged against the desk with a sigh. "No, it isn't Nyx. Where's her dimple?"

"Exactly. That was a bad mistake, turning the model to the right." I bent over, analyzing as best I could. "It's either her dress or an exact copy, but I'd swear that's a wig—there's too much hair. I don't recognize the shoes or handbag; she might have bought them recently—but I never knew her to wear anything but classic pumps in the daytime, and there are buckles or bows on those shoes, Flip."

He leaned over my shoulder, studying the photo. "I thought she didn't like Lanvin-Castillo," he said suddenly. "She went up in the trees over something they did for her, said she'd never set foot in the place again —so what's she doing there?"

"You see? It isn't Nyx."

"Why does she want us to think she's in Paris, if she isn't?"

"Not she, Flip—*they*, whoever they are. If Nyx

29

were engineering something, there wouldn't be a flaw —you know how she drives Props *crazy* with details. It's only because she's the best discipline in Hollywood that you can get anyone on a set with her.

"So she isn't connected with this, but why does *someone* wish us to think she's in Paris?" I picked up the lav key and peered into the gloom of the outer hall. "Which way do I go?"

"To the right, I think," he said absently. "I never use it myself . . . It has to be someone who hardly knows her, Katie. It wouldn't take more than a week or two for anyone to realize Nyx is as shrewd as she can hold together for anything connected with her career."

"Yes, I know she's wonderful—and will you stop rhapsodizing, and clear for action?"

"If she won't have me, how about you, Katie me love?"

"No thanks, Flip, you're only brother material to me." I did Nyx's little flip of the head and could hear him laughing as I went down to the door marked "Femina". When I got back, Flip was himself: brisk, organized, concentrated on the matter at hand. We sat over the notes from Nyx that were mostly business, but held useful titbits. "August, the porter, says . . ." "My maid Klara . . . her mother can rent two rooms, because Willi is in Bonn and Klara can stay at the castle . . ." "Found the set for wood scenes, riding with Kaspar—my horse is named Cronus, how suitable can you get!"

Every note would have to be memorized, because whatever the game, I had decided I could upset the applecart by taking Nyx's place. *They* wanted her to seem to be in Paris? They'd have some red faces and inconvenient questions from the Paris press when every Italian paper, magazine, TV and radio station was simultaneously photographing and interviewing Nyx in Rome!

"I've already started it, by accident," I told Flip. "I changed over in the airport washroom, in order to get in to see you without red tape, but it'll help."

"How? Nyx could easily be photographed yesterday in Paris, and today landing at Rome."

"Not disembarking from the *Naples* to Rome plane, Flip!" I chortled, while he was studying the *Figaro* picture again.

"Isn't that a clock?" He hauled out a magnifying glass, and it *was* half a clock at the right edge of the shot. The hands pointed to eight. "I think we've got something—that's a daytime shot, and this is the final edition. What's more, I'd swear I looked at *Figaro* this morning . . ." Flip tipped the wastebasket, scrabbled through the crumpled papers and disinterred the early edition of *Figaro*. It did *not* feature the picture. "Presumptive evidence but not absolute; they might have had the picture on hand for as much as 48 hours . . ."

"I don't think so; I bet it was delivered this morning, because the story they yanked was a real filler . . . somebody's two-headed cow!" I pointed out. "The instant they got the shot of Nyx, they used it, Flip . . . and the pix of me are on the wires right now, to gladden the heart of some editor on *France-Soir*! Let's back them up with generous coverage for Nyx in Rome: hit every contact you have for a press conference with Nyx at midnight. Split your list, I'll be your secretary—what's her name?"

"Carminelli . . ." Flip spun paper into his type-writer, dashed through his book and made a list. "Use her book for numbers . . ." Thirty minutes later we were finished. "Katie, you're a dream—I forgot you're the one with languages. If this blows up in our face, I'll hire you as my private, private secretary."

Between tension, and the hour, which was seven-thirty, the whole thing was amusing in spite of its seriousness. Finally, Flip mopped his forehead. "We need food—the one thing you *cannot* do is be tiddly at this conference."

"No, and there's another problem: passport. I can register on mine, you can hint I'm incognito, but as soon as Nyx is having a press conference, some film-struck file clerk is going to hunt up old fan mags, and discover Miss Hume should be Margaret, not Catherine."

"Damn, you're right, of course."

"D'you have a contact at the embassy?"

"Our Man himself . . ."

"Call him at once, say Nyx lost her handbag out of the taxi window in Naples, no time to hunt for it, so here she *is* . . . you'll plank her in the Excelsior on her sister's passport, but will he issue a duplicate at once? If he balks, remind him about vague movie stars —but he won't," I said. "People will believe almost anything of movie stars, particularly ambassadors, because they're so often involved."

It went as smoothly as whipped cream. His Excellency huffed a bit, but in the end, he came through. "If you use the sister's passport, what becomes of *her*?"

"She'll doss down in the Ladies'."

"Oh, nonsense! Tell you what, Hogarth: drop off a usable photo to Sanderson here, take the babes to dinner, kill a couple of hours. By the time you get to the Excelsior, he'll have the passport waiting at the desk —and don't tell me this road-company Alpha Centauri has to bathe and change and make up for three hours before dinner," Our Man barked commandingly. "For once, let her go as she is, you hear me?"

"Yes, *sir!*" Flip said respectfully, and I took away the phone before he recovered.

"I can't thank you enough, Your Excellency," I said in Nyx's unmistakable throaty voice. "If we'd ever met, you would know I'm not troublesome as a rule—and why haven't we met?" He was huffing more gently, now, and I said, earnestly, "It's only that I have a press conference tonight, but won't you and your wife stop for a nightcap after my stupid publicity bit, so I can thank you in person—about midnight?"

"Well, er, that's a pleasant suggestion, Miss— hmmm—Nyx," he grunted, "I'm not sure . . ." I could hear an agitated soprano twittering off-stage, His Excellency's harrassed half-muffled voice, "All *right*, Betty," and finally, "We'll try to stop in. If there's any difficulty, we'll be at the French Embassy, but I'm certain Sanderson can handle everything."

"Of *course*," I said cordially, "or he wouldn't be on

your staff—and I *do* look forward to seeing you later. I expect we've masses of friends in common. Thank you so much. Good-bye."

I replaced the phone gently. "That'll be a toughie to explain: Mr. and Mrs. Ambassador, rushing from the French Embassy to midnight supper with their old pal, Nyx!"

"Yes, a neat touch. Now what?"

"Find the photograph, reserve a table at Dell'Orso, call the Excelsior and order vittles for fifty people at midnight—I can do that . . ." While he dug around in the files, I was Miss Carminelli again, giving no details to the Excelsior, but hinting to Dell'Orso that Mr. Hogarth's guest might be Nyx . . .

"Is that wise, until you have the passport?"

"No one will want to see it in a restaurant."

He drew out an unretouched photo of Nyx. "They can crop for the face—but we can't go to Dell'Orso in street clothes."

"No, we can't. I'd forgotten that. Well, my luggage is in the gateman's cubby; I can dress in the lav."

"Well, I can't—no dinner clothes here. We'll have to stop at my place. Come on, we're tight for time, Katie."

We collected my handbag, his briefcase, turned off lights. As an afterthought, I scooped up both copies of *Figaro*, and we trotted down to—impasse. The porter's room was locked. "Break the glass . . ."

"No, let's try the hairpin first . . ." I had the flimsy lock open in a minute, while Flip scrawled a note.

"Or Pietro will have heart failure tomorrow morning . . ."

He went off to get the car while I dragged the bags into the yard and tried to relock the door. Needless to say, I was still twiddling when Flip came back. "Give it up, we're running late."

At the Embassy, Flip handed over the photograph, but Mr. Sanderson's expression showed clearly what he thought of careless film stars who lost passports out of taxi windows. He went away briefly and returned to accompany Flip down to the car, where he acknowledged our introduction with a supercilious squint—but he had the folder complete, needing only my fingerprint and signature. "Be careful until the paste dries thoroughly."

"Should I wave it in the breeze?"

"No," he said fussily. "This must *not* recur, Miss Hume. Really, I don't know what we're coming to . . . disturbing His Excellency . . . sheer carelessness . . ."

" 'Oh, my dear paws! Oh, my fur and whiskers!' " I murmured, irrepressibly, as Flip slid under the wheel.

He chuckled. "Never mind, it's worth losing ten minutes to have it in your hot little hand, but you have to dress *fast!*"

"Twenty minutes. Isn't it a lovely night?"

"Yeah—and I must be out of my mind," he muttered. "We don't know where she is, what's going on, what we're going to do—and I'm sitting here, letting you cook up elaborate plots."

"What else can you do? We'll be serious over dinner. Come on—I speak for the shower first . . ."

Pundit allowed me to pick him up; he did not kiss my nose, however, and when I said in Nyx's voice, "It's all right, old boy," he struggled to the floor and howled despairingly all the way to the kitchen. "Your cat is smarter than you are."

"How would he know? I think he's just hungry."

"Feed him by all means, but he knows I don't smell right."

"Perhaps you'll smell better after a shower?"

"To you, perhaps, but Pundit is not so crass," I said, insulted. "He knows I'm mighty lak a rose already; I'm just not *his* rose."

Aware of the cat's unwinking gaze, I braided my hair and pinned it temporarily. "Now d'you see—I'm Katie, pretending to be Nyx." I let him consider while I tackled make-up à la Nyx, which takes time, because she does lines and shadings for her eyes. By the time I'd finished, Pundit was sitting silently intent on the end of the mantelpiece I was using as pro tem dressing table. "Well, now d'you know me?"

"Waurrrw," he agreed, and padded forward to drape himself, stole-fashion, about my shoulders, purring vigorously. We went to the kitchen and talked to each other, while I found an iron and removed the creases from a dinner dress. I was just finishing when Flip bounced in, trailing the cord of his electric razor. "*Why* Paris?"

"I'm not sure. Maybe because she doesn't speak French."

Absently, he plugged the cord into a socket and went on shaving. "What has that to do with it?"

"Can't be Rome; you're here—not London: she can't have any trace of accent—and who goes to Berlin or Brussels or Amsterdam for anything?"

He turned away, tidily coiling the razor cord, but still *thinking*. I got out evening accessories, while he fumbled with cufflinks. "Why didn't that prince look after her?"

" 'Put not your trust in princes'," I rapidly buttoned shirt and collar. "Hold out your arms . . ." He stood there like an obedient robot, while I finished him the way Mother does up Daddy before a scientific banquet. "I don't get any of it," he said. "Why didn't she call me? They'd accept a collect call from Nyx, even if I were away."

"She might be someplace without a phone." I handed him a nail file. "Pundit, where's his tie?"

Pundit blinked briefly, padded to the right-hand closet. "Don't be silly, Katie; there isn't any place without a phone. The AT&T wouldn't permit it." I twitched an evening tie from the rack, averting my eyes from turmoil—thinking that if Flip and Nyx married, it'd be Greek meeting Greek when it came to untidiness!

"AT&T rarely installs in dungeons; they've hitched their wagon to Telstar." I slid the tie in place, evened the ends, had it butterflied and was perking the bow before he came out of shock.

"*Dungeons?*"

"Standard equipment for castles. Oh, *quit* it, Flip—of course she isn't in a dungeon. Put on your coat, brush your hair . . ." Pundit was sniffing delicately, to draw back with a Siamese snort. "After-shave lotion? Pundit doesn't think *you* smell right, either."

Wordlessly, Flip dribbled a few drops of Vetiver into his palms, patted his cheeks, dried his hands on a linen hanky, and arranged it in his breast pocket. He transferred wallet, money, keys, to his pockets—slid the wristwatch into place. "Well?" Pundit bent from the top of the chest and kissed him on the nose. "Okay, you're approved."

"What about you?"

"I'm approved, too. He knows I'm Katie, so it doesn't matter how I smell. Will you get a wiggle on, Flip?"

"Yes—and no," he said slowly, staring at me, his soft brown eyes suddenly dark. "You've conned me into getting you a phony passport, a press party— you've conned the American Ambassador into appearing for backing—but Katie, what's it all about? What in hell d'you mean to do?"

"Why, I'll go to Stelleberg and take Nyx's place, of course. What else?" I said. "Come on, Flip—Pundit, be a good baby while we're gone . . ." I tried not to show my fear. Dangerous as my idea was, it was the only thing I could think of to do. I was dreafully worried about Nyx; I had to save her . . . but what kind of weird tangle was I getting into?

Chapter III

FLIP LOOKED grim. "You're out of your mind—I'll call the police."

"What good will that do in Germany?"

"I'll get Interpol . . ."

"Why? It isn't a spy story."

"How d'you know, Katie? It has to be something more than Ring 'Round Rosy or A'tisket, A'tasket. We've lost her—how does it help if we lose you, too?"

"Flip, we're one up: *we* know she's in trouble—but *they* don't know we're onto it. By tomorrow, they'll know the Paris plan has flopped," I said soberly, "but we may flush something, all the same. Now hold everything until we're at table . . ."

I slithered from the car with a maximum leg exposure and extended a gracious hand to Tony, who hastened forward to welcome Nyx. I dawdled delicately, inquiring after his family, while flashbulbs popped—deliberately turning to the right, so the Hume dimple would be in every picture. I swept grandly into the main-floor bar, and by great luck, was able to nod sweetly to a couple of designers Nyx liked because they did marvels with costumes—and to register enchanted delight over an aging British star, sitting in dark corner with a boy who might actually *be* her grandson.

We were conducted up the fourteenth century staircase, leaving the pianist softly strumming "La Vie en Rose", and faced the middle dining room: dark green with a marble floor, and what passes for dance music in Europe—meaning you can't think because of the faint off-beat. I looked wide-eyed at Tony, who chuckled, "No, no—I remember!" and in a minute we were seated in the other dining room at The Table from which one can view the Giorgiones.

They were wasted on me, of course; I'm the musical one. To me, a picture is a picture—a mountain is a mountain; once you look, you've seen. But Nyx can look at Mount Monadnock, the Grand Tetons, anonymous sections of Adirondacks, Rockies, Alps, for hours. She says it is like contemplating her navel. I get the same effect from Brams' First Symphony or Bachianas Brasileiras, but apparently Flip was with Nyx. He sank into his seat with a deep sigh, and practically never looked at me again.

"What does Nyx order here?" Flip shrugged helplessly, so I smiled trustfully at the hovering maître d'. "I'm too tired to think. You know what I like, Tony. Surprise me, please?"

"Si, si—a specialty!" he beamed delightedly.

"Whew, that was smart of you, Katie."

"You won't think so when you see the bill," I

warned him, "and start calling me Nyx, for heaven's sake!"

Apparently what Nyx liked was a *large antipasto*, *a large* green salad, and something that started out as *fritto misto*, and turned into Sole Marguery, flambé with whiskey and a flourish of heavy cream. It was delicious, and a guaranteed nightmare producer. "No wonder I never knew what she ate," Flip said. "One glance and I'm bilious. How you *can*, sweetie!" He ate his own plate of scampi in silence, eyes chastely averted, and finally stated, "I am coming with you. That's that, and don't argue."

"I shan't. It's a good idea, if you can spare the time."

"What's more logical? Have to prepare for crew and equipment."

"Yes, but you will *not* stay in the castle. No," as he opened his mouth, "You'll be *outside*, with a well-publicized time for a daily phone call. The day you can't reach me, no matter what the excuse, is the day you raise the roof. You'd better have our code. For written messages, 'Having wonderful time wish you were here', unsigned, means 'Come quick, I need help'."

"So *that's* why you . . ." he muttered, "but the Paris wire was signed."

I nodded. "Another *bad* mistake. Listen, Flip: Nyx wrote the original card; she *meant* it. Someone decided it was safer to mail it than destroy it; it'd keep the sister lulled . . . couldn't chance signing, I might notice a disparity—but who looks at envelopes? Any reasonable facsimile will do—you open and discard.

"And that's what I did! They couldn't know that bromide was special to Nyx and me. It seemed so innocuous, they repeated in the wire, but for you, they signed . . . no handwriting in a wire; even the original form would be legitimately block-printed.

"Again, they couldn't know signing the wire was the clincher, *proving* to *me* that Nyx never sent it," I told him, quietly. "*I* knew she was not in Paris even before we found the *Figaro* picture, Flip. Nyx would never send that phrase, signed or unsigned, to anyone in the world but me. It's our private SOS, rarely used—but *never* used for anything else."

He nodded, frowning. "You said you kept in touch through me—mightn't she think I'd relay the wire to you?"

"Why, for such a commonplace? Because until now, you didn't know it had any significance for us."

He nodded again, "And so far as she knew, you were in Spain for another month, anyway."

"Exactly. If she'd wanted you to get in touch with me, she'd have sent something like 'Tell Katie need braces and bits soonest possible,' and *then* added the code, knowing you'd naturally read me the entire message—and *I* would understand."

"I see. What more?"

"On the phone, if overheard, we say 'Tweetie-pie'. Then the other one manufactures an instant excuse, like—she must leave the party because Uncle John only has an hour between trains, or I can't go camping on Snake River because I have to stand in for retakes."

"Face savers." Flip smoked silently for a moment.

"It comes back to me . . . once she phoned you, she said 'Tweetie-pie, I'm b-q'ing at Malibu with Flip,' and finally she hung up and said she couldn't go after all, because Uncle John . . ." His lips twisted. "You get it."

"I do indeed: no party. Where did you go?"

"I took her to Larue's; she had to eat somewhere—maid's night out and you were eating with your family."

"I *was?* You big fathead—shall I script it? She wanted to be alone with *you;* she alerted me, *I* provided a reason, *you* had a three hour tête-à-tête. You then drove her to the airport, offered to wait—she rushed in, rushed out in ten minutes with a sad tale of mistaken plane time, only a single kiss for darling Uncle John."

"Damn," he said violently, "*yes!* She even cried a bit."

"On your shoulder?"

"Of course."

"And you stayed until two, consoling her and drinking hot chocolate before the library fire?"

"Actually, it was nearer three before she was calm, and I suppose you haven't even got an Uncle John?" I shook my head sadly, and he broke apart. "All right, I was diddled—and I loved it. What else?"

"If we have to communicate anything anyone can oversee or overhear, we call each other 'sis', meaning 'ignore this.' If Nyx says, 'Sis, work out an interview on Monday,' it's for effect only; she can handle it. That covers everything."

"We better just add me, to keep it simple," he said.

"We use 'Tweetie-pie' for trouble and instant rescue; leave 'womderful time' as is, until she knows I'm in. Otherwise, it might confuse her; anyway, if we all use it, they might catch on that it means something."

"We can't use 'sis'; how about 'Flippy' and 'Nyxie'? Nauseating," I shuddered, "but people take *anything* from film stars."

"You're depressingly right, but *in extremis* you and I could use 'wonderful time' signed Flippy or Nyxie," he pointed out, thoughtfully. "I think that does it. Now what?"

"Study her letters and notes." We spread everything on the table, among the coffee cups, passing things back and forth silently. When we'd finished, we felt cheerful. For once, Nyx had been detailed, and my sister can write up a storm if she feels like it—because it's English, and description, and drama. Looking at the sheaf of paper, close-written on both sides, I had a fleeting wonder that she'd found so much free time—but it was all there, everything I'd need to go on with: names, dates, places, genealogical facts, thumbnail character sketches, humorous titbits and respectful recital of von Aspern family treasures. Combined with the notes to Flip, it was as good a briefing as anyone could have.

"When d'you want to go to Germany?"

"Day after tomorrow, I think . . . spend tomorrow at Simonetta, Perugia, lunch at Capriccio, dinner at Alfredo's, Bricktop afterward—all the photographs we can get," I said slowly. "I'm sure I'm right in scotching this Paris business, Flip, but something might break tomorrow that would give us a better clue."

"God, I hope so," he muttered. "I still say, police . . ."

"Not yet, but maybe later. Haste makes waste; let's not go off half-cocked, Flip—because the longer I think, the more clarity. You will, too. I'm changing my mind about Paris, for instance.

"If all they needed was for her apparently to have grown bored and left under her own steam, there were a hundred places to choose, all very anonymous and hard to check. Baden-Baden—motoring in the Black Forest—cruising up the Rhine—post-season at Garmisch-Partenkirchen. Then could have said anything; if you ever came back at them, well—that was where she *said* she was going.

"Why the photograph or wire, then? That would be the last thing wanted if she was merely to be *not* at Stelleberg!"

"If we think hard enough, maybe we can settle it here," he said, hopefully. "Okay, accept that there's a reason for *Paris* . . . I'll get onto the Sureté, say the photo is a phony, ask them to check for her passport entry anywhere last week. They ought to have that for me by tomorrow morning—but suppose *they find she did cross the border?*"

"Then they used her passport for the model, but if so, it was only at the border. The Sureté had no registration in Paris," I reminded him. "Ergo, the model is either French-born, or a registered French-speaking alien with a private home in Paris—and the instant you point *that* out to the Sureté, they'll Valjean it to the utter end. Very twitchy, the French, over passport frauds—and if Nyx is in Rome, confiding theft of her passport and replacement by Mr. Ambassador, whoever used her carte d'identité was bogus. I expect they'll turn up the model in jig time, Flip.

"Meanwhile, we will tentatively plan to fly to Wiesbaden day after tomorrow, where Nyx will gladden all hearts by a short appearance and a few kisses. You will arrange for a car, and we will drive to Stelleberg."

"I'm liking this less and less, hon." Flip shook his head, harassed. "Dammit, you two girls are no more fitted for international intrigue than Pundit—and I'm not much better. I *know* we've figured enough to satisfy us, but the whole thing rests on your ESP—and I'll believe it, but no one else will.

"And I don't see what in hell you can *do* at the castle. Are you meaning to prowl around and search the dungeons, or ask questions—because if they got rid of her, they're not about to admit it."

"There's a more vital point than that. How do I know Nyx is welcome to return to Stelleberg? As family guest, before the start of the rental contract, that is . . ." I remarked. "I don't know how they arranged her departure, you see, so one thing—tomorrow—is for me to try to reach the Princess, and judge by my reception whether I'm persona grata or not."

"You *feel* Nyx is alive? You feel she's nearby, under restraint, and angry?" I nodded. "Then with what we've got, let's break it wide open!" Flip clasped my hand earnestly. "I can pull strings, sweetie, get up to

J. Edgar and the Secretary of State, if necessary—pull rank, Interpol, if necessary . . . get everyone in the world asking 'Where is Nyx?' "

"You're not thinking clearly. If it was serious enough to shock and terrify her, it's serious enough for murder."

"They couldn't get away with it."

"On the contrary—only too easily, Flip. Depending on whether they used her passport for French entry, Stelleberg will say Nyx decided to go to Paris—or the Black Forest or wherever. She will have been seen in a car, driving through the village. If the model is found, she'll have a clean record and a straight story," I reflected briefly. "Her agent will be top respectable, will produce a request from Magneciné for a stand-in for Nyx. The model will be only one of several possibilities the agent arranged to be photographed—and the photo in *Figaro* will be due to an over-eager reporter."

"You make my blood congeal," Flip muttered. "It can't happen—can it? You're just making it all up, aren't you? How could Nyx get involved with anything like that?"

"I'm making it up," I agreed, "but d'you want to chance it? All they need prove is: she left Stelleberg. They'll be shocked, saddened, cooperative to the *n*th degree—and they can bury the body in the rose garden at midnight while the hue and cry works around Paris."

"*Don't!*"

"I have to, Flip—because the final touch, if Stelleberg become impatient, is the *coup de grâce*. Someone raises an eyebrow and murmurs, 'Hollywood publicity stunt?'—and right then, we'll have had it, sweetie. Oh, the police will take it seriously, when she never turns up. By then, it'll be too late."

"Assuming you're on target all the way," he said painfully, "*swear* you'll do nothing, no matter how small, without letting me know?"

"I'll promise for tomorrow," I said readily, "because I'm hoping for a break when they find the Paris scheme is ditched. Anyway, I want another day for both of us to concentrate, so I'll follow my schedule and we'll see what we've got at lunchtime and again by dinner. Come on, or we'll be late for Act I . . ."

I redid the swirling hairdo, remade the face completely, and stood before the long mirror, feeling unexpectedly nervous. I'd only done essential interviews for Nyx—such as when she was becalmed off Balboa and not able to explain because she ought not to have been there in the first place. Otherwise, Nyx always did her own work; I was no dogsbody for dull chores.

Tonight was different. Not merely that it was no fan-mag bit, it was my first foreign press conference and posed a special hazard because I couldn't react to anything but English or use any but basic polite foreign phrases. More than that, I couldn't go wrong by a hair, because this must convince the world Nyx was in Rome, not Paris—and establish conditions by which Flip and I could later hope to find and rescue Nyx before someone killed her.

Abstractedly, I wondered again what on earth she'd

stumbled onto that could make her death necessary, but there wasn't time to think now. Ten to midnight, and turmoil in the sitting room—Flip's voice directing lights, cameras, placement of food and liquor, sounding executive and faintly harassed.

Final check-up: Shoes? High-heeled, silly bows at heel and toe—okay, Nyx liked absurdities for evening. Dress? A bit ingenuous, but okay if Nyx were travelling. Jewelry? Ooops—Nyx never under any circumstances, *not ever*, wore a wristwatch. I removed mine and hunted out a couple of glittery evening rings, as well as a thin gold chain. Twisted twice around my ankle under the nylon stocking, it was a bit loose, but should pass in the crowd.

Earrings? Nyx and I had duplicate buttons: airy gold wire entangling chips of diamonds, turquoise, coral and seed pearls, given us by the parents for our high-school prom. No necklace to go with—but Nyx often wore no jewelry, and just as everyone was used to simplicity, she'd break out in a rash of diamonds. Tonight would be the simple phase.

I dabbed a drop of L'Air du Temps here and there, absently, but could see nothing glaringly wrong. Better not take the evening purse—compact, cigarette case, hankies, all monogrammed—remember Nyx smokes Chesterfields, won't compromise on English, translater if needed, but everything must be English . . .

Flip's voice, a tap on the door. "Nyx, are you ready?"

Now. . . .

I swung open the door and smiled radiantly. "Good

evening, how lovely to see you all, Flip darling, you'll tell me who everyone is, because *how* can I remember? I expect I've met every one of you—but then I've met every one of you in London, Berlin, New Delhi, Tokyo . . ." I shrugged apologetically and flashed the Hume dimple, and there was a ripple of laughter, while Flip's arm relaxed.

We moved from group to group, while they wolfed down canapés and Swedish meatballs. Evidently we'd caught everyone before he went to dinner, so he hadn't gone to dinner but was eating here— and while that spoke well for Magneciné's reputation, I couldn't help wondering how Flip would explain the costs on top of the Dell'Orso bill.

The questions were ordinary, at first. Flip introduced everyone very clearly, and if it were someone Nyx ought to know, he tightened his arm on mine slightly. By the time we'd circled the room, though, the pros had stopped eating and got out the notebooks —and almost at once we were in trouble.

My impressions of Stelleberg? "You'll see for yourself, when we finish the film—absolutely perfect background."

What was I doing in Rome? "Script conferences, casting, costumes," I widened my eyes in surprise, and someone murmured, "The side trip to Paris—perhaps for more personal clothes, such as a trousseau?"

A bit of a jolt to find they'd latched onto the Riviera interlude so swiftly, but the best defense is a good offense. "I haven't been in Paris," I glanced about. "Where's the man from *Figaro?* That picture this morning—I don't know *how* your people lent themselves to such a swindle, but there'd better be a satisfactory explanation and published apology, or I'll sue —and don't anyone smile!" I picked up the paper, and handed it to the nearest newshound, positioned myself, and said, "Tell me what's become of my dimple?"

The paper went from hand to hand and was convincing, while the Figaro man protested, "Merely a poor reproduction."

"It's not a reproduction, it's a *fake*, and you know it!"

"But at Stelleberg, they tell us you leave over a week ago for Paris."

"I shrugged. "A servant's mistake. I've been with my sister in Calabria, I flew here from Naples today, surely you already know that? Heaven knows they took enough photographs!"

"And you only register here at 11:30?"

"I was occupied with business details at Cinecitta, and if you must know," I retorted with a grin, "I changed for dinner in the *femina* and Mr. Hogarth escorted me to Dell'Orso, because when I'm hungry, I'm *hungry*."

There was another ripple of laughter, and Flip said humorously, "Ask me—and I'll show you how much she ate . . ." The atmosphere lightened into a froth of chuckles, waiters refilling glasses, and I found myself facing a weasel with glasses. He wasn't smiling. In the same voice that had asked about registering at 11:30, he said, very precisely, "Then your visit to Stelleberg is completed?"

"Forgive me—but who are you, please?"

"Vogel, *die Zeitung*."

Even if Nyx didn't understand German, she'd know the word for newspaper . . . "Which *Zeitung*, please?"

"Koblenz," he said sulkily.

"And what was it you wanted to know?"

"If you plan to return to Stelleberg, or perhaps," the guttural sneer was apparent, "it does not meet with your approval?"

"Of course it met with my approval, it's entirely perfect," I exclaimed, bewildered. "I'm looking forward to returning when we begin the film."

"And that date is?"

"July first," Flip inserted efficiently.

"Meanwhile you do not stay at Stelleberg?" Vogel persisted. "There is perhaps a reason—that Princess Adelheid does not suit your taste . . . or vice versa?"

Thank heavens I'd reread Nyx's letters! I took a good look at Vogel, and knew he was an *ist* of some sort—knew, too, there was method in his queries. "I do not at all understand your line of questioning, Mr. Vogel," I remarked, and with a sweeping glance, collected all eyes and ears on the interchange. "You seem somehow to have missed an installment in the serial—although it's only a minor business report, I assure you.

"I came to Europe for a vacation and to find a location for my next film. I met Prince von Aspern; when he learned I was looking for a castle, he suggested Stelleberg—provided we only needed two months, when Her Highness would be absent in any case. When he explained this to Princess Adelheid, she most graciously invited me to visit and see the castle for myself.

"It was never intended I would move in while Her Highness was in residence," I told Vogel impersonally, "but as it happens, Princess Adelheid has asked me to consider Stelleberg as a home, to come and go as I choose. I found Her Highness an enchanting personality. I assume, by her carte blanche, that she found me—acceptably well-mannered." My tone of voice left no doubt the Vogel would never make it, and there was a suppressed snicker in a rear corner, but mostly, the reporters were scribbling furiously.

"But as you should know, any film requires immense preplanning—so I left Stelleberg to meet my sister in Naples . . ."

"When and how did you leave Stelleberg?"

I allowed a long enough pause to focus all eyes on me. "I left at midnight on May 19th, Mr. Vogel, and I flew on a broomstick," I said deliberately. "I was wearing a black gown created for me by Morgan le Fay, and a hat that's got too small for Merlin. I had a black cat, but unfortunately he was a victim of acrophobia and the Finsteraarhorn was just too much. A pity," I sighed sadly, "he had a very pleasant purr . . . Any more questions, Mr. Vogel?"

There was a minute pause while he flushed an ugly dark red and looked at the floor—and the entire press conference broke apart in guffaws. Under cover of the noise, I said to Flip, "Tweetie-pie, d'you think you could check on that phone call to Hollywood? I'm dying to talk to mother—but with all this racket, we mightn't hear the phone unless you go in and shut the door."

"Right," he said, and disappeared. Definitely, Flip would be a valuable acquisition to the family—because there was no doubt Herr Vogel was purposive, and I'd not only evaded the traps but made a fool of him. Nyx now had a nasty enemy, and it wouldn't do to lose sight of him. He was already wiggling away around the outskirts.

"Mr. Vogel," I said loudly, looking about anxiously. "Where's my friend from Koblenz? Find him for me, darlings, I'm afraid he thinks I was rude—but you do know how it's irresistible. Don't let him leave till I apologize . . ."

They found him. They pushed him back into the middle of the throng, with rough good humor, slapping him on the back and assuring him in four languages that he mustn't be a touchy ass, he'd only got what was coming to him for stupidity . . . until he was facing me, blocked in by the men behind him, with no possibility of escape.

"Do forgive me," I said, softly abject. "Is it your first assignment? Truly, I didn't mean to make it difficult." I was getting through to the others, but Vogel's eyes were tiny flickering steel points behind the thick glasses, darting this way and that, a hunted animal. *So I was right, he was here to check up . . .* meaning a tight organization, because they couldn't have known Nyx was in Rome before I came out of the airport at half-past three. *Interesting . . .* how'd they pick it up fast enough to get Vogel here? A cadre in Rome, who knew Nyx couldn't be here—or a picture in one of the German evening papers, that led to a quick phone call to the Rome agent? It would be simple for anyone to discover Nyx was at home to the press at midnight—no doubt there were a dozen other free-loaders, gorging the free lunch and pretending to take notes.

Vogel was different. I slid my hand through his arm and patted it gently. "Forgive me?" I said again —and could smell the musty odor of sweat in an uncleaned suit. "Have you any more questions? Go ahead, ask them."

"*Nein, nein, keine frage,*" he muttered.

"I'm sorry, I don't understand . . ."

"I have no questions," he said loudly, pulling free of my hand with such force that I toppled against another reporter, who said, "Hey, take it easy, man," and gently pushed me erect again. "Damned hun," he muttered under his breath. "You okay?"

"Yes—but I think he's had too much," I muttered back, urgently. "Please, I hate to bother you, but would you see him home for me? Let me know where he lives? You see the spot I'm in: a *German* correspondent—and I want that castle for the film . . ."

"Sure, I'll baby-sit—what's in it for me, to take him home and give you his address?"

"One drink tomorrow at five—and I promise not to press charges against whoever brought you here for supper," I murmured sweetly. "What's your name?"

"Neil Robinson, and I didn't come for supper; I came to see Nyx," he said. "If I get five minutes alone for playing I Spy, it'll make up for five months in Vietnam!"

Vogel was beginning to struggle, thrusting forward and being repelled by large reportorial hands, voices admonishing, "You don't treat a lady like that."

"Oh, let him go, boys. He said he hadn't any more questions."

They let him go, moving to surround me laughingly, while Vogel scuttled away through the people beginning to drift into the hall. I could see Robinson quietly sliding in pursuit, as Flip emerged to say, "They're putting through your call, Nyx."

"Oh, I shall have to go," I breathed. "Mother's birthday—but there aren't any more questions, anyway."

"Just one." It was a swaggering Irishman, top man for a syndicate, who'd had a few but meant only to tease. "There's no truth to the rumor that it was not you, inspecting Stelleberg for a suitable film location —but you being inspected by Princess Adelheid for a suitable daughter-in-law?"

"And I didn't make the running and was booted out? Sorry," I chuckled, "but no truth!"

"Maybe *you* couldn't take her?" he joked.

"Now *that* is a vile canard, and if Prince von Aspern doesn't sue, I will!" I laughed, shooing with my hands. "Do go away and stop manufacturing romances, like fan magazines!"

In the general shifting and racket, I sensed a new note—a making way, respectful bowing, and Flip bringing forward Mr. and Mrs. Ambassador. Oh, hell, I'd forgotten *them*, and now they'd arrived late, they'd probably stay late, when I needed to think.

They came forward on a tide of goodwill, and they were so happy to meet Nyx, so delightfully normal and home, that I was immediately undermined. Flip was pushing people out of the way and positioning cameras, and Mrs. Ambassador and I were already giggling together. His Excellency was caught in the bonhommie, so the camera got some superb shots of him with his arms about both feminine shoulders, while we were apparently doubled up with glee over a reunion.

"Heaven knows what the barbarians have left us," I said, to Mrs. Ambassador. "It's been a *madhouse*. Flip, sweetie, sweep the rabble into the dustbin and send for a Welsh rabbit or something, so we can relax peacefully," but Our Man was already surrounded by the top-top newshounds, avidly firing questions ad lib. "Oh, *doesn't* he do it well!" I said admiringly.

"He's had plenty of experience, but it really is too late," she said, half-flattered and half-anxious. "I wish he wouldn't!"

"Oh? Well . . ." I got up and said firmly, "Party's over, everybody out—shoo, vamoose, scat. No, no arguments; you came to see *me* and you saw me, and there are no dividends. You will now leave quietly by the nearest exit, so I can talk to my friends. Goo'bye, darlings—lovely to see you, see you *again* sometime, and *off* you go . . . *shooooo!*"

Laughing, shaking my hands, snitching the last canapés, the reporters moved toward the hall door—in which stood a man.

He was *tall*, six foot two—or four—maybe *six*; he

practically filled the doorway. From the corner of my eye, I saw chiseled features, thick dull gold hair in lazy waves, shadowed eyes and total impassivity.

Oh, NO, I told myself desperately, *it can't be— what would he be doing here?* But even while the reporters streamed past him—and I was lighting a cigarette for Mrs. Ambassador (who asked to be called Betty)—and Flip was rounding up stragglers and alerting waiters for fresh provender, I knew I was facing the firing squad.

So far, I'd been able to turn so I never faced him directly; could I make it into the bedroom, catch my breath, think what to say? "Will you excuse me for a minute, Betty? I'm *hagged*—I need a dab of powder . . . want to come with me?" I nearly made it, but His Excellency turned from a jovial farewell to the diehards, and in a ringing voice, said, ruefully, "Damned if I didn't forget—and here he is waiting at the door! Nyx, we were rude enough to bring an uninvited guest from the dinner party—but *you* won't need introductions: Prince Rupert von Aspern."

Chapter IV

"Rupert!" I whirled about and hastened forward, hands outstretched in incredulous delight. "What a heavenly surprise, darling! You can't suppose you should apologize, Your Excellency; I *told* you we'd have masses of friends in common. Oh, lovely to see you, Rupert—I had no idea . . ."

His hand held mine gently, he bent over with a brilliant smile—but the eyes were cold with anger. Behind him, Flip looked ready to faint as Rupert said, "Nor I—but surely I told you I'd be in Rome?" His voice was a deep baritone. "A most welcome surprise to me, also—when all the time I'd understood you were in Paris."

"No, I was *never* in Paris, darling; we can none of us understand this picture," I said, tugging him toward a chair. "Sit down, do—Flip, get some food, sweetie? I'm famished—worn to the bone . . . let me freshen a bit? Betty . . ."

"Have you been in Rome, then?" Soft, steely, insistence . . .

Wide-eyed incomprehension, faint frown— "What

are you talking about, Rupert? You knew I was motoring in Calabria. I just got in, to discover this *odd* thing about Paris. Flip, I need cigarettes—see if they've Chesterfields, will you?" I pushed Mrs. Ambassador ruthlessly into the bedroom. "Back in a minute," and shut the door firmly.

And as clearly as I'd ever felt anything about Nyx in my life, I *felt* hurt, puzzlement, almost a cry "How could you?" Betty was chatting lightly of nothing in particular, and I took a deep breath. The apparent ESP for Rupert was only guilt at fooling him. For all I knew he was behind the whole thing—although, if so, why should he be angry, and by his eyes there was no doubt he was seething. I felt a bit temperish, too. Dammit, why did he have to show up before I was ready for him?

I redid my hair, powdered my nose, added a drop of perfume, and arranged to meet Betty at Simonetta next day. "You mustn't let me *buy* anything. Harry's having an economy fling," she mourned, inspecting my cosmetics with interest. "Somehow I thought a film star would have more, not that you need anything at your age. Oh, L'Air du Temps, d'you like this?" She sniffed delicately, "Mmmm, nice—may I?" dabbing generously.

She was a real darling, natural as a teen-ager, poking among the lotion bottles. "You must certainly have met dozens of film stars before," I said, amused.

"Of course; they crawl out of the walls, but you're different. You're not a Creature. My, it'll be fun to see what Nyx orders, even if I can't have anything—

but then," she cheered up slightly, "it'd be mutton dressed as lamb on me. *Promise* you'll remind me, if I start to get carried away!"

We came out laughing, to find the men laughing, too: Rupert, glass in hand, evidently dramatizing something, while His Excellency relaxed on the couch and Flip chuckled over the bar tray. "What *are* you doing, Rupert?" Betty slid past him, to sit beside her husband. "Oh, is that coffee—may I have some?"

Rupert stood suspended, and again I felt bewilderment, as Betty said, "Go on, Rupert, I didn't mean to interrupt."

"I'm sorry, I forget where I was, it was nothing important," he said. "Nyx, would you like coffee, also?"

"I've earned a drink! Nothing is more exhausting than a press interview—and how well you all understand!"

"Of course, but what I do not understand is the mix-up about Paris." Rupert suavely took the drink from Flip and brought it to me.

"Oh, no more do we, darling," I assured him, wide-eyed. "I met the Challoners in Naples, we trotted around to Taranto, were going on to Bari, but Moira has a *back* and those country roads were too much, so we headed for Naples. Pure chance I came straight on, and *there* is this picture of *me* in Paris, on the front page of *Figaro!*" I looked impressively at Betty. "I was *thunderstruck*—but it's being investigated, never fear."

"By George, *I* remember seeing that picture in the

final edition," Harry began, "just before . . ." Flip looked faint again, but fortunately Betty cut in, "Are you related to *Professor* Hume, Nyx?"

"My father."

"Everybody was talking tonight about the Paris Congress," she babbled. "Are you flying up to be with him? You must be sinfully proud, Nyx, such a fabulous mind! Oh, Harry, *stop* the Top Secrecy, Rupert was *there*, the Hume *family* certainly knows —you don't seriously suspect poor *Flip* of being an enemy agent!"

"Well, no," Harry said confidentially, "but it's still *confidential*, Betty."

Daddy in Paris? So *that* was why Nyx had to seem to be there! By Flip's expression, I knew he'd got the same answer. "Actually, I didn't know; I expect Mother'll tell me—if my call ever goes through. Flip, do check again?" He nodded, closed the door to the bedroom. "What is it, another decoration?"

"He's head of the Science Section of the United Europe Congress, officially opening tomorrow." Rupert's voice was toneless. "He's been there several days, unofficially—and you say you didn't know?"

I shook my head. "Unwritten family rule: never talk about Daddy, never ask questions, forget anything you hear—which is why I deliberately forgot you were coming to Rome, I suppose. Automatic reflex."

"Damned good rule," Harry grunted, still a bit miffed as Flip called, "Nyx, it's going through now."

"You'll excuse me? Really meant for Mother's birthday, but now I must ask about Daddy, too." I went hastily into the bedroom where Flip was saying, "Mrs. Hume, one moment . . ." Taking the phone, I hissed, "Close the door, keep going, in five minutes open *wide* with a message about Katie, so everyone hears me talking." He nodded and vanished. "Mother, I'm in Rome."

Oddly, despite her absorption in Daddy, nobody can fool Mother. She said placidly, "Are you, darling? Are you enjoying it, how lovely of you to phone, is Nyx with you?"

"No. Mother—you and Daddy can *talk* to each other, can't you?"

"Yes," she said after a moment.

"As soon as I ring off, tell him: no matter what he hears, what messages he gets, *he must ignore it. Nyx is NOT in Paris.*"

"I'll tell him. Why? Is there trouble? Where is she?"

"I don't know. I *feel* she's safe, but someone is trying to make it appear she's in Paris: telegram to Flip and a news photo—but it's only a model in a wig. I couldn't think *why* Paris, but just now I heard Daddy's there, so I think that has to be it, don't you?"

"Oh, definitely! It was absolute hush; I'm surprised you heard."

"Slip of the tongue from the Ambassador's wife, but of course she thought I'd know where my own father was."

"At the Merciers, if you want him," mother said absently. "Are you being Nyx, Katie—because I feel you should be *very* careful, darling. Where will you be?"

"I think I'm going back to Stelleberg. That's where she was; seems a logical place to start. Flip's got the Sureté working the Paris end, and the Ambassador and his wife are here now, *with* Prince von Aspern. They dined at the French Embassy, which is how they knew . . . Mother, off the record, what's Daddy doing and where—because evidently someone knows."

"He'll be at the Congress until Sunday, then he goes to Bonn for talks with whoever wins the June First elections."

"What can I say, officially? They know I'm calling you . . ."

She reflected. "You can say Daddy has the honor of reading the opening speech, and it's expected he'll be elected Presiding Officer. Will that do?"

"Marvelously. Oh, Mother, I do love you!"

"I love you too, darling," she said quietly. "You can't know what a comfort it is to Daddy and me that you're in charge of Nyx—but I think, if she can get into a predicament that might involve Daddy, you had better *tell* Flip to marry her."

"I already did this afternoon; he'll ask properly as soon as we find her." The door opened. "Wait—he wants to say something."

"My love and best wishes," he said, "and I had a card from Katie; she says she's going Doge-hunting in Venice."

I relayed the message in a bubble of mirth, while there was that unconscious respectful silence for long distance in the sitting room. "Mother, darling—many happy *happies*—love to Georgie and Sylvia. I won't call Daddy tonight, it's too late—perhaps a wire tomorrow. Good night, darling."

"Darling yourself," mother snorted, amusedly. "So it's my birthday, is it? Where's my present, wicked one? Katie," her voice suddenly sober, "I *think* you can do it—but I *feel* serious danger. Be very careful, child!"

I rang off, went back gaily. "What time? Late enough! You made a slip," I told Betty. "I'll trade: Daddy's to read the opening address—and he'll probably be chosen Presiding Officer. What d'you think of *that?*"

"Great!" His Excellency beamed, expansively.

"A well-deserved honor. So you fly to Paris, after all?"

"No, of course not, Rupert. Daddy doesn't much like family underfoot when he's working—and Betty and I are going to Simonetta."

"Oh, *no!*"

"She only wants to see what a film star orders. Please?"

His Excellency arose majestically. "My wife doesn't need to see what a film star orders; she's forgotten more about spending money on toggery than you've had time to learn, young lady. Come along, Betty. Nyx," he shook my hand warmly, "it's been a real pleasure. How long will you be here?"

"Haven't had time to plan," I began, but Rupert cut in smoothly, "You fly back with me tomorrow. I insist. Mother would never forgive me for not bringing you with me." His eyes were implacable despite the smile.

"*Must* it be tomorrow? I *do* have chores, Rupert."

"So do I—but if we leave at four, we'll be home for dinner."

"Good lad," His Excellency approved. "Take her away before she and Betty bankrupt us—not but what it'll be a near thing if they have until four. Couldn't you make it earlier—say, nine a.m.?" He turned to the door, chuckling, sweeping Betty and Flip with him. "You've your car, I suppose, Flip—Rupert, drop you at the Embassy?"

"Thank you, but as it happens I am staying here, so I shall be rude enough to outstay my welcome and finish my drink."

Flip hesitated. "Those script changes, Nyx?"

"Not tonight, Flippy; run along, you've been a Trojan, sweetie." I kissed him casually on the cheek and stood waving in the doorway. *The best defense* . . . I shut the door, leaned against it. "Now—what's the matter, why the annoyance?"

He looked at me impassively, swirling the liquid in his glass. "Disappointment is a better word," he said slowly. "I didn't think you—a garden variety Hollywood actress, Nyx. Nor did my mother—and to pack and leave with no more than a message via a servant . . ." He shrugged and swallowed his drink. "My mother is philosophical; she understood it could not be entertaining to sit with her over needlepoint, but she was—disappointed, all the same, because you'd seemed to enjoy this.

"My annoyance, as you term it, is a dislike that my mother shall be disappointed," he finished. "She would never ask for an explanation—but I do." He was angry enough now to stride over and fix another drink without asking permission. I stood still, and as I hoped, the silence goaded him.

"We spend the dinner hour making plans for a boat trip, and to visit the castle of our cousins in Weiningen; you even suggest a picnic in the woods," he controlled his voice with an effort, "and the next morning when Princess Adelheid von Aspern sends word to *her guest* that she will be ready to drive in an hour, she learns *from a servant* that Fraulein Hume has departed at six in the morning, saying 'Thank you very much, I am going to Paris'."

There was a long pause. "Will you fix me a drink, too, please?" I sat down, thinking furiously: Nyx was abducted at night, her luggage gone—but in his resentment at the slight to his mother, how deeply had Rupert investigated? I looked at the tall handsome man bringing me a highball glass, and I felt certain his accusation was no act. Immersed in thought, I said, "Thanks," took a sip and spluttered involuntarily.

"I *thought* I remembered—scotch and soda with plenty of ice . . ."

"Yes, it's only this filthy European soda," I said, because I'd forgotten; Nyx does take soda. Rupert's eyes flickered slightly, examining the bottle, "It is the same brand we use at Stelleberg . . ."

"Somehow it tastes different, perhaps a different bottling plant." Gritting my teeth, I sipped again. "Sit down, Rupert, because something is extremely wrong."

"At first, I thought it was merely clumsily done," he said evenly, "but I knew your father was coming to Paris. I supposed you'd gone to meet him, not realizing you could tell *me* . . . and tonight, I learn first that you are in Rome; later that you knew nothing of Professor Hume's participation in the Congress. You have, in fact, been touring Calabria with friends! Isn't it natural that I wonder you were not gracious enough to say this was planned, and you preferred it to the Stelleberg plans?"

"Entirely natural," I agreed, "but on my side, I'd left a very long explanatory letter for your mother and had not the faintest idea you weren't fully aware I was in Calabria.

"It *was* sudden—and probably American informality, to feel that since none of the plans was definite, all could be deferred," I said apologetically. "I woke about four, I think—out of cigarettes, so I paddled downstairs looking for some. The phone was ringing, there was no sign of August—*naturally* I answered.

"It was Katie—and she's American, too, so it never occurred to her there'd be only one phone in a castle," I said earnestly. "I'm sorry, Rupert—but she *needed* me." Oddly, I could feel I was getting through unexpectedly easily. If he'd asked *why* she should *need* me at 4 a.m.—but he only nodded silently, as though this was quite acceptable. "So I packed—wrote a letter saying I had to go to Calabria with Katie, and hoped she'd permit me to bring Katie back with me . . ."

"Where did you leave the note?"

"On the incoming mail tray, to go up at breakfast," I said promptly. "When Katie arrived with the car from Frankfort, I piled in and left, never dreaming my letter would be lost."

"It was reported someone was trying to reach you by phone," he said slowly. "We instructed August to say what we believed true: that you had gone to Paris."

That wasn't the message Flip ever got, I thought. "One call was me, in Naples, asking you to hold any mail—but August couldn't understand at first, and then we were cut off. Any other calls were Flip, trying to say he had to go to New York—but I don't understand what became of my letter."

"Nor I—but it was not found; Klara presented herself to my mother, saying August had told her you had gone to Paris."

"Curiouser and curiouser, because there was no one about when I left, Rupert. Where could August have heard *Paris?*"

"That's to be determined when we get home, of course."

"Considering you're disappointed in me and feel I've been rude to Her Highness, why d'you want me back?"

"Shall we say, because she has liked you, Nyx—and she has not much to amuse her these days," he said after a moment. "I had the impression you liked her, also, but if you find our life too leisurely for your tastes, there's no more to be said. I should not like her to be—distressed a second time."

Cleared of anger, his eyes were an incredible deep sapphire blue. "What time shall I meet you tomorrow?" I asked, half-hypnotized. "Last minute possible, please? I do have chores."

"Four-thirty latest, earlier if you can." He tossed off his drink and rose, smiling down at me. "I won't apologize for adding to your exhaustion," he said softly. "It had to be straightened out, did it not? You know what it means for us never to misunderstand each other, *liebchen*." He pulled me gently to my feet, walked me to the door, his arm about my shoulder.

"Of course," I breathed automatically, concealing inner shock. What was the relationship between Nyx and this man, for heaven's sake? *Good God, could they have been lovers? No*, or he wouldn't now be leaving. I felt *limp* with relief, while he opened the door and pulled me to face him, turning up my chin in one hand.

"*Gute nacht, meine herze—schlaf' wohl*," he murmured, and kissed me full on the mouth.

Involuntarily, I swayed forward and abandoned myself to his arms—what's a kiss, after all? Two minutes later, I pulled free and said, dazedly, "Rupert, you *must* go, darling, or I'll never manage everything before meeting you. Good night."

He stepped back, his eyes suddenly *bright* blue, and said in German, "You are so beautiful, you rival the stars, my darling, and I shall love you till I die."

I was still bemused, staring at him blankly. "What *are* you saying, sweetie? You know I can't understand a word."

His eyes darkened slightly. "Only wishing you a good night's sleep," he said, after a moment, looking at me intently. "Tomorrow . . ." He blew me a kiss, smiled and went down the hall, to vanish at the staircase without a backward glance. I could hear him whistling, *Zwei Herzen im Drei-viertel Tag*, on pitch and in perfect rhythm, receding down the stairs and finally gone . . .

I threw away the scotch and soda, fixed a proper highball with water, and telephoned Flip. "I have to be at the airport no later than 4:30—which means you have to do some things, Flip, because I won't have time. Paper and pencil, please . . .

"New luggage—mine is monogrammed; Xerox copies of all notes and letters—large quantities of *cash*, first thing in the morning—I'll make a list of simplicities like make-up, send your secretary to buy them. Tell the Sureté Daddy is staying with Professeur Louis Mercier . . ." I spun through my address book, gave him the street number, "they can tell Louis *anything*. I'll meet you at Capriccio at one for progress report."

He said "yes" to everything, sounding dazed, and I was about to ring off when he came to himself and demanded, "Are you all right, Katie? He didn't try anything, did he?"

"Only a casual good-night kiss . . ."

But of course Rupert *had* tried something: he'd spoken to me in German, *knowing* Nyx wouldn't understand it, and not translating correctly. He'd kissed me good night—and if that was the way he was accustomed to kiss my sister, I could only feel *devastated* for Flip.

Sliding into bed and staring into the darkness, I realized I felt a bit devastated for me, too.

Chapter V

PROBLEMS, PROBLEMS, in every direction: what to say about Nyx's original luggage, presumably taken with her to Calabria . . . *why* was Katie now in Venice, when I'd just been on a motor tour with her? Had I really convinced Rupert—or was he pretending to be convinced, in order to further his own plans? I couldn't make myself believe he was part of whatever was going on; he'd never have given an imposter so many helpful bits of information . . . unless all he'd said was untrue, meant only to entrap me?

Most of all, what was the status between him and Nyx?

Judging by the kiss he'd claimed almost as a matter of course, they were only a half inch from a full scale *affaire*—and I didn't believe that, either. Or perhaps I didn't want to believe it, because I'd thoroughly enjoyed kissing him—which was a hell of a note if he were slated for brother-in-law. Fond as I was of Flip, I hadn't the slightest desire to kiss him beyond a peck on the cheek.

If only I could talk to Nyx—but try as I would, I

felt nothing, and eventually the concentration sent me to sleep.

Flip arrived simultaneously with breakfast and a sheaf of newspapers. Nyx had gotten major coverage; *Figaro* had even used the shot with the Ambassador, which amounted to tacit apology. The Sureté had nothing final on the passport; they'd reached Daddy early in the morning. "Dubois says he already knew Nyx wasn't in Paris, but he's detailed a man to stay with your father until things clear up."

"That's nice, but I don't think they mean any physical harm, or they'd have gotten rid of Nyx."

"We don't *know* they haven't, *and they still could!* If you show up, they might use you for an alibi," he groaned.

"If all they wanted was an alibi, they already had it with the *Figaro* picture, and have it even more after last night," I pointed out. "No, it's directed at Daddy. If I'd known he was in Paris, I wouldn't have placed Nyx in Rome; we'd have lain low and let Daddy catch them. It's too bad, but they still don't know he's alerted, so there's a chance."

Thinking of the press conference recalled Vogel. "See if there's a Zeitung in Koblenz, and a reporter named Vogel—and you'll have to meet Robinson. I'll write a personal note, but *make* him give you Vogel's address."

That was the most frantic morning. Luckily I'm a stock size, but Betty was a complication. I ordered a few gowns to be sent after me, but she was still startled at the speed with which I bought off the peg. Understandable that Nyx couldn't be leisurely because of Rupert, but she was still faintly let down. "Next time we'll allow three days," I promised, and she brightened slightly.

"Maybe next time I can buy something, too," she said, hopefully, "although I never knew a time my allowance wasn't in hock—but if I knew in advance, I could try to save until you come." She kissed me affectionately. "You're a dear, exactly what I thought Nyx would be. Your mother is so lucky. I always wanted a daughter, but all I got was three boys, and somehow—oh, I don't hate their wives, but they're all from Boston."

The taxi pulled away with a final wave of her hand, and it was a wild scramble thereafter: Perugia, the glove shop, everything taking far too long because Nyx didn't speak Italian, and was always generous with autographs.

Flip was already waiting at Capriccio, and had been smart enough to order lunch, but he was a bit taut. "Nyx's passport was used on May 25th, at a country village near Sarreguemines—a limousine, about three a.m."

"That figures," I nodded.

"How?"

"She only speaks English," I said patiently. "At any major entry, someone speaks English, will wish to talk with the glamorous Nyx, want an autograph—and notice an accent. So they pick a back road, catch a sleepy border official who may be unable to speak anything but French or German. Five will get you ten the model turns out to the Alsatian."

"Damn, you're frightening, . . . Nyx! As it happens, she is. They haven't found her, she's evidently skipped, but you were right about the agency: Øltgren is tops, girl's name is Rosa Martineau, been with him for years, one of his best models." Flip consulted his notes. "Born in Wissembourg, thirty-five years old, a natural blonde, but all measurements agree with Nyx, so for a stand-in job, she only needed a wig.

"You missed on the instruction wire, it wasn't from me, but from Nyx—a long day letter from Wiesbaden, May 19th, and since it was delivered, the original form was discarded. Same with the wire to me from Paris: handed in at the busiest office at the busiest time—safely delivered, original form discarded.

"The photograph was delivered by messenger to *Figaro* at eleven a.m., apparently from Øltgren . . . whose developer says he found the roll on his desk when he came to work, plus the usual memo of instructions—only his prints on it, no connection between him and Rosa.

"He made two prints as usual, and an extra of what seemed the best shot, as instructed! He went for *café complet* around 10:20, leaving the pix on his table, returned twenty minutes later, and separated them into a file set and a set for Øltgren. The extra was gone, and he supposed a secretary or errand boy had picked it up—but no one admits this, Dubois is inclined to believe them."

"Is there a well-known flirtation between the technician and the receptionist?" I asked, thoughtfully.

Flip snorted. "Dubois says if you ever need a job, see him; they could use you," he remarked. "*Of course* the receptionist alway enjoys her *café complet* with Paul-Edouard, and a *fiançailles* is momentarily awaited."

I shrugged. "Rosa got the picture, plus an agency envelope, hired a kid for a franc to deliver it to *Figaro* —you'll never find the kid short of advertising. If the pix of me at Rome airport hadn't hit the evening papers, she'd still be wherever it is she lives."

"10, rue Boissonade, Left Bank," he said absently. "One thing you haven't guessed: Dubois says she was once married to a German named Johannes, last name presently unknown. Øltgren understood she was divorced; the concierge says not—the husband was occasionally there, she supposed he was M. Martineau— but always the same man, speaking French with a German accent."

"Who telephoned late last night," I said, "Rosa was in seventh heaven over a marvelous vacation, packed and flew away on wings of song about midnight?"

"Not quite. Oh, there was a phone call—in German, which the concierge doesn't understand. Rosa emerged from the booth, white-faced, *maman* was ill . . . she must leave at once—but Rosa is not in Wissembourg, nor is her mother ill."

"Of course not; Rosa is with her husband, somewhere in the Mainz-Wiesbaden-Frankfort area," I said absently, "and he's connected to Stelleberg in some way. I may find out when I get there, but if the Sureté can get cooperation from the German police, they should be looking for a Frau Somebody, who's

76

been away, is now returned from nursing a sick mother."

"I'm sure Dubois will welcome your analysis," Flip murmured sardonically.

"Don't be nasty, Flip; I've been more right than wrong so far, and the hell with Rosa—what're your plans?"

He concentrated on a mouthful of canelloni. "You're really going through with this: three hours alone with that guy? Anything could happen; we never planned on this. I meant to take you to Frankfort, drive you to Stelleberg and be sure you arrived, but now," he shook his head, troubled, "how do we know you'll ever get there?"

"I don't think Rupert's in on it. Why take me back, if he knows I'm not Nyx? I wouldn't know whatever makes her dangerous; why give me a chance to learn? He could so easily have put us in an impossible spot, Flip—taken the position, in the presence of our Ambassador, that since I'd ended my personal visit, I would naturally not return before start of filming. Then what could we have done? Instead, he's played directly into our hands."

"How can you expect to fool him for three hours, when you only fooled me for ten minutes?"

"He hasn't known Nyx so long or well as you— and he knows nothing about me," I said slowly. "Easy for you to know she can't carry a tune, Flip, but he mightn't know it, as yet . . . nor how closely we resemble each other. He was puzzled and angry last night, but not suspicious. His story was logical; your presence and the press conference would confirm I was Nyx—unless he knew I couldn't be, which brings us back to the beginning. He doesn't know."

"All right—but I'm on the six o'clock jet," Flip stated uncompromisingly, "and I'll actually beat your time, so I'll phone from Frankfort around 7:30 or 8:00. Tomorrow I drive out at noon, so Nyx can show me the terrain. Eat up and let's go; you still have to pack . . ."

In the taxi I hastily skimmed through the Xerox copies, and found that Nyx had mentioned Rupert flew an Aero Commander, placed at his disposal by Bonn. There was a private airstrip at Stelleberg . . . he meant to show her the aerial view of the Rhine when he had time. From Rupert's instructions on parachute, safety hatch, oxygen mask, I gathered the trip had never occurred—so it was not necessary for me to pretend knowledge I didn't have, thank goodness.

He was entirely different today. Apparently he wasn't one to hold a grudge; last night was finished and forgotten. He was blithe and happy as a boy, smiling and jovial, his eyes unclouded, clapping Flip on the shoulder and cordially inviting him to stay at the castle whenever he came for final scheduling.

We took off a few minutes after four, climbed to 8,-000 feet and flew northwest at a steady 300 miles an hour—and as many times as I'd flown this course, it was a new pleasure to be not too high to *see*. It was new, too, to be in a private plane with a handsome pilot who evidently meant to be as charming as possible.

Once on course, Rupert relaxed and smiled, reaching for my hand. "Nyx, *liebchen,* so good to have you back! Mother is delighted; I told her this morning we would arrive for dinner. She sent her love and said I should tell you the silks have come."

Silks? "Oh, wonderful—was she pleased with the colors?"

"Yes, she was bubbling like a girl, to have them waiting for you." He squeezed my hand warmly. "Such a *clever* suggestion, darling! Mother so enjoys needlepoint, I don't know why she never thought of an old-fashioned sampler before."

"Perhaps it's not such standard child training for princesses as little American Victorians?" I said lightly, overcome with relief—because Nyx can design and drape on a dress form, but my stitches are neater and more even than hers. "I have my great-grandmother's sampler framed in my room; I always meant to copy it, if I ever had time."

"Tell me about it."

"Oh, it has the alphabet and numbers—and a frieze of birds and animals around the edge. I suspect the governess did most," I chuckled, "because everything is very straight except the name: Catherine Louisa Suydam, and the date, April 12, 1839. Those stitches *wobble*—but after all, she was only four."

"She may be forgiven, surely?" Rupert laughed and squeezed my hand again. "Now tell me what you did today? I hope you didn't permit Betty to buy anything?"

"No, but we've a date," I said mischievously. "I'll

79

let her know, she'll save up—and we will spend three days shopping."

"Oh, poor Harry!"

"He can afford it, he's filthy rich: Texas oil and cattle ranches besides."

"Ah? I thought you only first met last night, how do you know his financial position?"

"One of the ranches marches with Uncle Randall's. I forgot that last night, darn it; I should have reminded him," I said absently, peering from the plane. "Oh, is that Firenze?" When it was lost behind us, "I forgot to ask: how do we go?"

"Milano, Locarno, Domodossola, through the Simplon to Thun, Berne, Basel and straight home." He fiddled with a few buttons and levers, and calmly pulled me against his shoulder. "Pay attention to me, please; I will tell you when to look again."

"Is this wise?" I asked, flustered. "I'm not much for one-hand driving even in cars, Rupert."

"But here there is an automatic pilot, so it is entirely wise and highly enjoyable," he inhaled deeply against my temple. "You have a new perfume," he observed, sniffing as delicately as Pundit.

My heart plummeted: oh, *stupid* to forget Nyx was addicted to Nuit de Noel! Damn, he was smarter than I'd thought. "Yes, L'Air du Temps, Betty persuaded me. D'you like it?"

He sniffed again, ending with a fleeting kiss. "Pleasant, but I think I prefer the other—what was it?"

"Nuit de Noel, but I broke the bottle in Naples and thought I'd try something new—but I can send for a replacement."

"No, no, it's entirely pleasant," he said again, "merely that you smell different, darling. Ah, we come to Milano . . ."

Again I was glued to the window while Rupert talked efficiently to local controls. I fancied I could see the Duomo, a building that might be La Scala, then we were past and I was overtaken by a mammoth yawn. "Sorry," I apologized, horrified, but Rupert only chuckled.

"You've had an exhausting two days, *meine herzegeliebste*," he agreed, reaching for my hand again. "Close your eyes for a bit."

"Oughtn't I to talk to you, keep you awake?" I asked, but he only laughed and said in German, "No, I am the pilot, I never sleep but watch over you always, beloved."

What a pretty thought . . . My eyelids drooped—and suddenly flew open: *Nyx doesn't understand German.* "What did you say?"

"Only that I am entirely awake, never fear," he said presently. "Go to sleep." Later, he roused me. "Time for the mask."

"Where are we?"

"Approaching the Pass—then Blumlisalp, Jungfrau. We go past, not over, but in this plane one must use the mask at 10,000 feet." Drowsily, I felt his hand efficiently checking me . . . settling his own mask . . . felt the plane lifting, lifting. Only twilight below, but still sunlight surrounding us—catching a snowclad peak in the distance, a drift of mist swirling forward beneath the plane, so that we seemed floating on a sea of whipped cream, alone in the world

. . . alone in the world . . . "Nearly home, wake up, darling!"

It was full dark outside, now. The mask had been loosened while I'd slept. With a single blink, I felt totally wide awake and refreshed. Unconsciously, I peered at my wrist, and remembered Nyx doesn't wear a watch. "What time is it?"

"Just seven—and there we are." I could see flood-lights springing up about the strip. Rupert circled once, then we were down so smoothly I scarcely felt contact, taxiing to a stop and surrounded by smiling faces, while Rupert swung himself to the ground.

Standing among the men, he was obviously a prince, a born leader, and deeply loved by those who served him. I slid to the open door. "Rupert?" I placed my hands as he had done and swung down—into his arms as he dashed forward to catch me.

"*Die albernheit!*" he grunted, setting me upright. "They're bringing down the steps—you might have broken a leg, you silly child!"

"Not me, darling, I never break anything—and it's so good to be back. I'm dying to bathe and dress, look over the silks—and we mustn't delay dinner too long, even if we are returned wanderers." I smiled broadly and waved my hand to the attendants, while a jeep was rushed forward, skidding to a stop before us. The driver sprang out, to be replaced by Rupert; I clambered in—the bags were piled behind—and we were off, bouncing in and out of curves and woodlands, until at last we turned into a main drive and I *saw* the castle.

It loomed, it beetled, there was a moat and a drawbridge—but it was still somehow a kindly castle, twinkling with hospitable lights. "August will be at supper; could you manage your dressing case?" Rupert asked, unloading the other bags.

"Of course—and your attache case and the small shoe bag."

"Thanks." He fumbled briefly, swung open the heavy door, and we stood in a square hall, with a broad staircase leading up to a landing that split into side stairs beneath a magnificent stained glass window. There wasn't a soul in sight. "If I take up your bags, can you manage alone?"

"Of course," and thank heaven for someone to point out Nyx's room!

It was the second door in the right corridor; Rupert took his attache case, hefted his own valise and trotted off to the left corridor with a final smile, while I shut my door.

The room was immense, immaculate, silent but for a tiny fire. I found a bedside lamp and rapidly opened luggage, dug out dinner clothes and the travel clock: 7:35. No time for a bath if I were to do a proper make-up. Dozens of doors: what was the bathroom? One was locked, evidently connecting to the next room—four were closets, one was a sort of make-up room, probably originally used for powdering wigs! Finally I found a door leading through a narrow hall lined with linen shelves, to a gigantic bathroom, that must once have been a bedroom itself.

No time to explore. I dashed back and forth, creaming my face, stripping off travel clothes, dragging fresh hose, underwear, shoes from my bags, with no time to put anything away. There were two huge wing chairs facing each across the big fireplace—*terribly* in the way. I pulled them back to the wall on either side, leaving a clear passageway, and in twenty minutes I was ready.

I stood before the great triple mirror meant to frame a Mauve Decade beauty, but I was only a Twentieth Century imposter, wearing a clinging silk dress of *bleu de pervanches*, fantastic mobile earrings strung with fake gems, my hair in Nyx's swirl caught with glittery combs. Was I going to get away with it? I took a deep breath, said "Now!" and opened my door.

Coming swiftly to the landing, I faced Rupert in dinner clothes, whistling softly to himself and trotting downward, arranging his evening handkerchief. At sound of my dress slithering against the balustrade, he looked up and for a moment his face was still, his eyes intent. "Nyx, how beautiful you look! One of the new dresses?" He extended his hand to assist me. "A magnificent choice, darling—it intensifies your eyes."

Well, that was why I'd bought it, of course. "I'm glad you approve, sweetie, and even happier I'm not last down." I tucked my hand in his elbow confidingly and together we descended, turned to carved double doors standing half open, so that I could see the baronial hall that must be at least fifty feet long—if it were properly proportioned. In the center fireplace there was a brisk fire. Beside it in a straight-backed armchair that towered like a throne sat a white-haired woman holding a glass of sherry and reflectively smoking a cigarette in a Denicotea holder.

She was Gladys Cooper, Catherine Nesbitt and Sybil Thorndike rolled into one, and you'd have known anywhere that she was a true princess. "She's so lovely," I said involuntarily, pausing at the door.

"She says the same of you," he murmured, and swung back the wood panel. "Mother, here is your present from Rome."

She turned toward us eagerly; Rupert's same deep-set blue eyes were faded now, yet still sparkling happily. "Nyx, my dear child," her voice was thin, precise in pronunciation, "it is so good to see you." Her hand reached out, beckoning gracefully, and I sped forward over the silky old Chinese carpets to bend down and be gently kissed on the cheek.

"Equally good to be home again," I said, sinking down on the ottoman before her and aware for the first time of another figure.

A man, in dinner clothes, standing on the far side of the fireplace, staring at me ashen-faced, his fingers trembling so uncontrollably that a few drops of wine slopped over the edge of his glass, and he sought to recover by tossing off the remainder at a gulp.

Even before Rupert came forward to kiss his mother in his turn, I had the missing link.

Kaspar . . .

Chapter VI

"KASPAR, *wie gehts?*" Rupert said heartily, and I smiled brilliantly, too, still holding Princess Adelheid's thin fingers in mine, and recalling Nyx's letters.

"How are the drills? Is Thoma still walking with two left feet?" I smiled into his eyes again—and by the flicker of frightened incredulity in his gaze, it was settled: this was the man who knew I was not Nyx, *because he knew where she was.* It would take a while to figure what I might know, how dangerous I might be, but so far I had the drop on him.

There was a small hubbub of chit-chat. "Nyx, the usual?" "Oh, may I have it very light and on the rocks, please? I seem to be getting used to that since Calabria . . ."

"Was it a pleasant trip, did you enjoy being with your sister? Why didn't you bring her with you, my dear?"

"She wanted to visit friends in Venice—she says she is Doge-hunting."

"I am glad to have you to amuse me," Her Highness smiled, "but I confess I am eager to meet this

Katie whom you say I shall find even more *simpatico*," as Rupert brought my drink, looking anxious. "I hope it's all right, I didn't realize you no longer wanted soda."

"Oh, I'm part chameleon, I change constantly, didn't you know? Kaspar, where's your drink? I expect a toast to the wanderer's return—and another for the embroidery silks."

He was pulled around now, setting his glass on the tray. "Could we drink later? I must telephone to delay tonight's drill," he smiled ruefully. "Good to have you back, but it throws the schedule off a bit."

"Tell Hansi to take over, Kaspar; for once you won't be missed, and I've things to discuss after dinner."

"Of course, but I must still telephone, excuse me . . ."

It was too late. Already, a pleasant-faced old man with grizzled hair and myopia was tapping at the door, "A telephone call for Fraulein Hume."

"I'm so sorry, but I'll make it short," I apologized—and remembered Nyx had described August as the prototype of "Dat l'il old winemaker *me*." I went to the door, "August, how are you?"

"I can't complain, Fraulein, and I needn't ask about you—more beautiful than ever!"

"Oh, August, you need glasses!" I patted his arm à la Nyx, and closed the library door firmly on his chuckles. The room was silent, dim-lit. I sped to the phone on the desk. "Flip?"

"Yes, you're okay?"

"Yes—the one we want is Kaspar," I kept my eyes

on the hall door that was so far away in the shadows. "No questions, get someone onto it, observing some sort of drills tonight—check a sidekick named Hansi, give me your address and phone number." Was that ornate handle turning ever so slightly?

"Colonel Forster, 22 Rheinstrasse—Wiesbaden 6245," he said. "My God, Katie, *Kaspar?* You mean they're *all* in it?"

"No, it's solo." I could see the door shimmering in the lamplight—inching open. "Darling, too marvelous you're here, bless Flip for telling you! I'll be waiting for you at noon, *heaven* to have a sight of you! I must ring off, darling; someone wants the phone and we're late as late for dinner."

The door was closed, the hall empty aside from old August, bent over a newspaper in the porter's cubby. I went back to the great hall, but from my seat it wasn't possible to watch the entrance to the library. Eventually, Kaspar returned and we were moving into a medieval banqueting hall for dinner, although by a clever placement of screens, and a normal-sized table set before one of the fireplaces, it was made to seem intimate. There was an elderly butler named Wilhelm, and a waitress named Maria, who apparently doubled as family chef.

The conversation was principally between the brothers and concerned the election next Monday. Princess Adelheid said little, but listened with deep interest. From Kaspar's eyes, I knew Nyx was still wherever he'd stashed her, but he was playing it very cool, smiling and eager in the discussion with Rupert.

Covertly I studied Kaspar: some of the family good looks, but not well-defined. His hair was wavy, but plain light brown; his eyes were a chill light gray, the nose a bit thick, the body stocky, where Rupert handled his height with grace. Kaspar was a Teutonic burgher; I suspected a dash of Viking blood in Rupert. Still, they were identifiably brothers, and they seemed close, companionable, while Kaspar was making quick reports: who would supervise the polls, who was getting out the vote, who would tally.

"Well, it seems you've done your typical thorough job, Kaspar," Rupert said finally, smiling at me. "This is my right-hand man, now—couldn't manage without him."

"Obviously," I smiled back, as we left the dining room. "I expect he already knows who's going to win."

Kaspar turned away quickly, but not before I caught a flicker in the gray eyes. "It's the people's choice," he said, and Rupert slapped his shoulder affectionately, "but we may suspect you've done your best to influence that choice," he chuckled.

"Naturally," Kaspar admitted, humorously, "but don't quote me!"

We disposed ourselves about the coffee table, laughing, and I'd forgotten to put a hanky in my evening bag. "I must run upstairs—pour my coffee, please, I'll be right back . . ."

The bedroom was silent, still an untidy mess, but even as I found a clean handkerchief, I sensed *difference*. Something was not as I'd left it—what? It had not been Klara, Nyx's maid—she'd never have left things draped over chairs . . . Chairs! That was it.

I'd swung the heavy armchairs close to the wall, in order to move freely. One was now pushed away—aligned to the wall, but not against the fireplace. Someone had been in the room . . . an emissary of Kaspar, hoping to identify me, of course. But every scrap of paper was hidden in a brocade pochette now reposing in my evening bag. I felt weak with relief, but there was still the *reason* for that displaced chair.

Why move only that one? I'd left nothing on either chair. It was easy to see under and around, and nothing lay in the corner. Standing close, to peer into the corner, I dimly heard sounds. I laid my ear to the stone; fantastic it might be, but certainly there was a staircase in the fireplace?

A thrill of fear ran through me! I ran my hands over the carving, searching for a spring. Nothing else explained the chair: it was not meant to be there blocking entrance, and the searcher had disarranged it in opening the door and couldn't replace it in his retreat.

Not a house servant, then, or he could have left openly; it had to be someone who couldn't explain his presence in the hall should August happen to see him. My fingers caught a shell-shaped carving and felt movement. I pulled—and a two-foot section swung out silently.

I was so relieved I could have laughed! There was nothing secret about the spotlessly clean hall and circular stone steps lying before me, lighted by utilitarian flex with evenly spaced unshaded bulbs—not a sinister shadow, cobweb, spider or rat anywhere. I propped the door open against the chair, and reconnoitered. In the depths of the castle I could see shadows moving, hear cheerful chatter, giggles.

Nyx's abduction route, probably, but also obviously step-savers for the castle servants. Used by family, too—for I could hear ascending footsteps and Kaspar's voice. I fled back to close the door and push the armchair in place again, hearing the steps coming steadily nearer, a jaunty whistle passing my door and finally, a dull thud followed by silence. So Kaspar's room was next to mine? Thoughtfully, I turned off the light and went down to find Princess Adelheid sitting alone over her embroidery.

"Rupert asks you to excuse him, he has gone to work with Kaspar in the library," she smiled. "And there is your embroidery, if you are in the mood; Lise kept it carefully."

"How kind!" I picked up the fine canvas and I could *feel* Nyx at once. It was apparently a pillow cover, not large enough for a chair seat, and silk petit-point unsuited for a footstool. The design outlined in colored pencils was Nyx at her best and most fanciful, but with suppressed amusement I knew she'd enjoyed that more than stitching. She'd done no more than a few inches. Unconsciously I glanced at my hostess's work.

"Yes, I shall finish first," she said mischievously, "but then I have been working steadily. Tell me about your trip; I have never been to Calabria."

"First, I must apologize for American thought-

91

lessness," I said earnestly. "We are so used to spur of the moment—but I should have remembered it is different here. Rupert was seriously provoked with me."

"Not for long, I'm sure," Her Highness smiled, "and no apologies are needed. I'm happy you were able to return. How is your sister?"

I picked up the needle and automatically fell to work, chatting about Calabria and the Challoners, with an occasional comment or question from the Princess. At last Wilhelm produced a tray of bouillon steaming over a warmer, flanked by thin chicken sandwiches, and we laid aside our work.

"This is the nicest custom you have taught me, Nyx," Her Highness remarked. "I cannot imagine why I could not think of it for myself—all those years of hot milk, and," firmly "I can *not* like this Ovaltine."

"Nor I!"

Leaning forward to set the empty cup on the tray, she studied Nyx's embroidery. "What a lot you have done in one evening," she murmured, admiringly. "I must look to my laurels or you will catch up to me."

Ooops, she *was* on the ball! "Never fear! Fun to do the figures, but I shall bog down over the background."

"I shall retire," she announced. "If you mean to wait for Rupert, we'd better have another log to the fire."

"I think not tonight, it's been a hectic day. I'll be glad to get to bed." We went up together to the landing, where she kissed my cheek softly. "Good night, my dear. *Schlaf' wohl!*"

"You, also," I said warmly. Her eyes sparkled slightly, but she only turned away to the other corridor with a final wave of the hand and disappeared behind the first door. As it closed, I could hear her gentle voice saying, "*Lise, müde bin ich heute abend . . .*"

Well, I was tired, too—and my night wasn't over. There'd been no second search; the chair stood as I'd left it. I pulled it away, opened the door an inch and heard only silence—but the lights were still lit. Were they always on? No, there was a wall switch on my landing at the head of the stairs.

I kept awake by hanging up, putting away, setting empty bags in a closet. I removed make-up, had a bath, crawled into slacks, sweater, tennis shoes, and settled down to wait. At half-past one the staircase lights were out. I turned out my light and propped the door with a wad of paper. If the lights went on, I'd see a glimmer—but by the time I'd smoked four cigarettes, and the luminous clock dial said 2:30, there was no sound or light.

It was unlikely there was any regular night watchman, and absurd to think Nyx was anywhere in the castle, but if the staircase in the stone walls of Stelleberg was used daily, she must have known of it, too. Cautiously, I stole out to the landing, leaving my door faintly open and the bathroom light on—there was just enough light to be certain of finding my own door.

Gripping the pencil torch I used at the screening of Nyx's rushes, I went quietly down. A single door on the lower landing must lead into the main hall—another flight of stairs and a totally ordinary back door of heavy wood with a glass upper pane . . . even more ordinary kitchen, pantry, serving stairs. All was immaculate, silent, closed for the night. As a segment of a horror movie, my nocturnal journey was a *bust!*

No doubt once these were part of the castle defenses. There would have been a guardroom for the soldiers, and probably a few dungeons, but today the springs were unhooked, the secret doors no more than swinging panels. I yawned mightily and was about to return upward, when the tiny light hit a heavy door in the opposite wall to the kitchens. *To the dungeons!* I thought excitedly, and found I was right.

There was first a large square room with a disused fireplace. I could imagine a bunch of swaggering toughs in the Stelleberg uniform, quaffing beer and dicing at a wooden table while prisoners languished beyond, but these days firewood was piled high along the inner wall. Wooden shelves across the outer wall held thrifty preserves, pickles, home-canned fruits and vegetables. The air was chill, a perfect temperature for storage. I shivered, but couldn't resist a peek at the dungeons.

There were six on each side of a hall, their iron bars either removed or pushed open: whole hams and flitches of bacon hung over supplies of spirits and liqueurs; there were trunks, traveling bags, an ancient pigeon-breasted dress form—the stuff one usually puts in an attic. I went to the end, and the last two cells were locked, containing steel filing cabinets and transfer cases—important family and estate records. One cell was full; the other held overflow. I'd turned and moved away when something registered.

I swung back to the overflow room, steadied the torch, and I could see the edge of rawhide luggage behind a file cabinet—or I thought I could. The lock was ancient, only secured for the sake of formality; you could practically have inserted a finger and turned the thing. I got out the hairpin, and in a twiddle the bars swung back.

All of Nyx's luggage was piled behind the cabinet: six matched pieces, monogrammed beneath canvas travel covers, and the small dressing case she hand-carried without a cover. They were disguised by a filthy tarpaulin, but it had slid aside a few inches—and I had seen the edge of the dressing case.

It took the best part of an hour, but eventually I got every case upstairs, emptied them onto my bed, and replaced the bags. I hadn't much hope but I tried, anyway—and for once I was lucky; I managed to re-lock the barred gate. Sticking the hairpin back into place, I thought that *this* should give Kaspar furiously to think!

It was five in the morning before I'd finished putting everything away. I pulled the heavy draperies and tumbled into bed feeling unexpectedly confident. Nyx was nearby, at least within reach of a telephone, since Kaspar had been able to check in only a few minutes before dinner. I thought happily of his confusion when I appeared in Nyx's clothes—and more soberly, I considered what it all meant. Neither Rupert nor his mother was aware of any undercurrent. Tricky as it was, I felt I'd passed with flying colors, despite tiny things like different perfume.

If only I could keep my head, be alert for a word or look of surprise, surely I could continue to fool two people who hardly knew my sister, after all. I had no compunctions about it. If anything, they ought to be grateful if I retrieved Nyx without scandal . . . which left the original question.

What was Kaspar up to?

Chapter VII

I woke to infinitesmal sounds: Klara—it could be no one else—stealing about, mouselike, in the shadowed room, tidying ashtrays, placing a vase of fresh lilacs on a chest, laying out fresh underclothes . . .

"Klara?"

She hastened to stand over me, beaming delightedly, a fresh-faced village youngster, still carrying some puppy fat. "*Ja!* Iss zo gut you komm back!" Nyx had liked her, taken pains to help her uncertain English. "Bath?" she asked. "I bring breakfast then."

"Thank you very much." I slid out of bed while she pulled back the draperies to bathe the room in brilliant sun. Lying in the tub, I felt energetic and confident. I still didn't know where Nyx was, nor why she was dangerous to Kaspar—but logically it must tie in with these elections. Yet *how*—and why should it involve Daddy?

Could it possibly be a tempest in a teapot? Say Nyx had developed some ridiculous disease—measles, chickenpox, something bad for publicity; Kaspar whisked her to a nursing home, and clumsily tried to save her face by that business of Rosa Martineau in Paris? Rupert knew Daddy was in Paris, but I'd a hunch he was like Daddy: really wouldn't reveal a word, so perhaps Kaspar didn't know and the choice of Paris was accidental.

Somehow it didn't jell in my mind. Still, it was a possibility. I crawled from the tub, patted dry and went out to find two notes on the breakfast tray. "*Liebchen*, I regret—something unforeseen, I must go to Mainz today, see you at dinner. Have a happy day, darling—Rupert."

The other note was a stilted repressed handwriting. "Nyx, you will do me the honor of riding at three as usual, please? Kaspar."

As usual? Hmmmm, if the situation was innocent, surely I'd be told during our ride. "Klara, tell Prince Kaspar I'll meet him at three."

"*Ja*, I haf riding habit ready," she nodded. "*Die Prinzessen sagt*—says," she corrected herself with a giggle, "she meet you at *mittagsessen*." She debated with herself, "*was bedeutet mittagsessen?*"

"What time and where?"

"One and a half, in eating hall."

"Luncheon, at one-thirty," I translated, smiling.

She sighed hopelessly. "You teach better than I learn, Fraulein."

"Never mind, you learn faster than you think," I soothed, while she brushed my hair expertly into Nyx's swirl. She giggled happily and went away to clean the bath while I concentrated on make-up. I was just finishing when she returned, astonished. "So long you take today!"

"I was thinking of something," I said evasively, throwing down the powder puff and standing up for the suit jacket she was holding.

"New!" she said appreciatively, smoothing the pink linen over my shoulders. "From Rome? Iss beautiful!"

"Thank you. By the way, Klara, what made August think I had gone to Paris?"

She hung her head. "Iss terrible mistake, all my fault, Fraulein," she said humbly. "You are telling me you will go to Paris for costumes; when room is empty, I think I have not understood—you have been saying you go *now*. I ask August, who says he not see, but he hears car . . . so," she shrugged, "we are stupid: we say what we think we know. Forgive me, Fraulein."

"Of course, there's no harm done," but I wondered: How had Kaspar meant to explain Nyx's disappearance—if he'd not had the good luck of Klara's bumbling?

There was a rap at the door. "*Herr Hogarth die Fraulein sehen will.*"

"Yes, I'm coming. Good morning, August—Klara, tell Her Highness I will meet her at luncheon . . ."

Flip was waiting at the wheel of a dun-colored Volkswagen whose only quality was that it *ran*. We whizzed over the drawbridge, that had apparently been in place for so long it was doubtful it could ever be raised again, and turned left. "Where are we going?"

"Find the first likely-looking hidey hole and park; I

have to be back by one-fifteen." Obediently, Flip found a narrow side road, pulled us bumpily under a weeping willow. "Now, you first," I said.

"Vogel is a waiter at the German Embassy," he began. "Robinson read your note, and he's cut himself *in*—gave me a spiel about Vietnam and your picture in the barracks, and ended up, 'Nyx's in trouble; you go to Wiesbaden, and I'll handle this end'." Flip looked at me worriedly. "I didn't admit anything, but what'n hell could I do, Katie?"

"Nothing but be grateful, and he may turn up something. So Vogel is attached to the Embassy? Interesting—but I don't think it was Kaspar who told him to check on me. What else?"

"Forster says there's considerable unrest over these elections, rumors of an upset; he's digging into these drills you mentioned, but they seem to be just boys' clubs, little kids about ten or twelve years old." Flip consulted his notes. "Nothing more from the Sureté, except that your father hasn't been approached; they've still got a man with him, in case . . . The German police are cooperating on Rosa; so far nothing. That's all—what about you?"

He went pale green at the gills while I related the inner staircase, Nyx's luggage, the search of my room, "Not Kaspar, he was right under my eye, and fortunately I had all passports and letters in my evening bag, so they couldn't have found anything.

"One thing: I still think it's political, although I don't know how Nyx got involved in a mystery—but it *could* have another explanation." I outlined the theory of accident or illness, and a clumsy cover-up unconnected with Daddy. "Klara's story seems to fit, you see?"

"What about my last phone call, when they were apparently relaying messages back and forth," he objected.

"Yes, but again—it wasn't August or Klara, they don't know a thing, but suppose it was Kaspar himself? It *could* still fit—a quick try at getting you off their necks."

"Katie, for God's sake—you can't go riding alone with this guy!"

"He won't try anything; he only wants to see what I know—and perhaps I can find out what *he* knows . . ."

On the dot of three I was walking toward the stables, and one question was answered: Nyx knew of the inner stairs. Once into my riding boots, Klara calmly opened the fireplace panel. "Enjoy the ride," she said carefully, and giggled.

I trotted down, waving to Maria in the kitchen, and went slowly along the path. Nyx knew which way the stables were; I didn't. Rounding an immense syringa that looked like a giant snowball, there was a choice of paths. I settled for one that led over a rise, and could see Kaspar standing beside a saddled horse, talking to a man in rough tweeds. From Nyx's letters, he would be Hansi, the estate steward who doubled as stable master.

I hastened forward, smiling. "How are you, Hansi? Kaspar, I'm not *very* late, am I?"

"No—and if you were, you know quite well you'd be worth waiting for, Nyx."

"Darling, how Chesterfieldian of you!" I said throatily. Everything about the setup told me that Hansi was in the plot. He ducked his head, unsmiling and sour-faced, muttering indistinguishably.

"*Nicht Cronus, mach' schnell*," Kaspar returned casually. "Where shall we ride?"

"Where you like, I feel agreeable today. What a pity Rupert couldn't be with us!"

"Yes, he is too often confined by political matters," Kaspar agreed, regretfully, "but perhaps tomorrow. Ah, here you are."

I looked at the handsome chestnut tossing his head and high-stepping toward me—and if ever I saw a horse that was fresh, he was *it*. "Oh, not Cronus?" I said, disappointed, and was rewarded by a startled glance from Hansi to Kaspar. How did I know? So whether or not they'd identified me, they didn't know Nyx's sister understood German: Point one for our side.

"Cronus has cast a shoe," Hansi apologized, "but you will find Stellen-jager equally comfortable, Fraulein." Now he was all smiles and politeness, giving me a leg up while Kaspar swung into his own saddle. I looked at Hansi's nasty little pig eyes twinkling with satisfaction, and realized something else, as the chestnut snorted and sidestepped after Kaspar's sedate bay.

Nyx is a riding academy horsewoman, capable of sitting a rocking horse, no more. I do her riding sequences, unless they're stunts—because I learned to ride in Texas. I once covered Uncle Randall with glory by hanging onto a colt for a full forty seconds at a local rodeo! I leaned forward, quietly. "Hold everything, and we'll play when we reach open ground, d'you hear?" He tossed his head, whiffling impatiently, but a bit more controlled. I brought up alongside Kaspar. "Stellen-jager—what a pretty name, what's it mean?"

"Starlight," he said, eyeing me covertly.

"Pretty in English, too," I exclaimed delightedly, knowing he was probing. This was bound to be the wicked horse in the stable; Stellen-jager means "place hunter."

Did they mean merely to frighten—or hope for a fatal accident? How, and when? We trotted along, chatting peacefully, but I was alert and waiting; my horse was waiting, too. The move, when it came, nearly caught me off balance, even so. Kaspar's compliments grew more intimate.

He was making love to me! I couldn't believe Nyx had ever permitted or invited this, and my face must clearly have revealed shock. "Please don't, Kaspar," I said automatically, as he leaned to catch my hand.

"*Ach*, Nyx beloved," he returned passionately, "what has happened in Rome to make you so cold to me? It is Rupert! He has turned you against me!" He'd talked a shade too long; I'd freed my hand by the time he brought his horse against Stellen-jager and, lunging for my hand again, cleverly grazed the chestnut with his spur.

That was *it*. Stellen-jager threw up his head with a scream, danced wildly and bolted. We were headed straight across a field, toward a hedge, another field and woodlands beyond. This horse was really a hunter! I got ready to jump and called, "Good boy! Throw your heart over and let's go!"

We soared over like birds. By the time we were down, he wasn't bolting, just enjoying himself with the exercise he'd been needing. There seemed a dirt road, running beside the fields and turning off into the woods, but I thought I'd better not let him. The horse was still needing a run, which would be dangerous among trees. Accordingly, I steered him left and we tore completely around in a wide circle.

Academically, I wondered how Kaspar would get out of his failure to rescue "Nyx beloved". Now I could see the panorama: Kaspar, apparently thrown by his horse who'd been upset at Stellen-jager's bolt, and just now struggling to his feet. . . . but his horse was standing peacefully, about a yard away, daintily nibbling grass! Wickedly, I rose in the stirrups and waved joyously. He was pretty far away, but I thought he looked dazed . . .

Stellen-jager and I went around again; by now, he was feeling *much* better, entirely happy with both of us. "Let's see the woods?" He whuffled agreeably, and we trotted forward, while I told him what a magnificent fellow he was. The woods thickened, but there was only one road, evidently well-used. So long as we didn't hit a fork, it was safe enough.

Behind us, there were rapid hoofbeats and Kaspar dashing up to us. "What are you doing?" he demanded angrily. "You *know* it's a rule that no guest enters the forest."

"But you're with me. Couldn't we go a bit farther?"

"Absolutely not! There's no time; we must turn back at once. Nothing to see, in any case. The road goes only to the wood-cutting." He grabbed the bridle, forcibly jerking Stellen-jager around. "Really, after this—all I want is to get you home in one piece. *Ach, Gott!*" Kaspar launched into the alibi: distress, despair, near heart failure, imminent tragedy. The Story, in fact.

I listened with *deep* interest. "When I saw this beast bolting, with you—and Klinge stands on his hind legs and throws me . . . *me!*" he said, anguished. "I cannot come to your aid . . . I hardly dare to look, and when I nerve myself—it is to find you serene as at a tea party, even disobeying The Rule." We were back to the outer field, Kaspar turning along the road.

By Stellen-jager's snort, I knew he wasn't satisfied. I'd guaranteed a run; he'd only had half of it. Kaspar was still building The Story, "I fear a serious reaction," he said, and turned, startled that I wasn't pacing him. "Why do you wait? Please, Nyx—I cannot understand you at all today!"

I gave him her wide-eyed ingenuous stare. "Can't you? Truly, I didn't mean to be difficult, but," as his eyes flickered with fury, "I think Stellen-jager and I will go as we came. See you at the stable!" I waved casually, flicked him gently with my crop and said, "All right—*go!*"

In a split second we were headed for the hedge . . . we were over, landing like velvet and romping down the home field, immensely pleased with each other. "Enough for today, tomorrow we'll do it again!" I could hear Klinge's hooves racing along the side road, but we'd come the short way and were placidly prancing into the stableyard long before Kaspar.

Hansi's face was a study when I slid down and went to pat Stellen-jager's nose. "We came through the fields," I said gaily. "No more Cronus, please; this is my boy." I dug in the pocket of Nyx's riding jacket and found, as expected, a hoard of sugar lumps. "There, then! Tomorrow we'll have a real gallop, eh?"

Kaspar cantered into the yard, pulled up short. Leaping down, he grasped my shoulders anxiously, "Are you really all right, Nyx?" He glared at Hansi. "There was nearly an accident! how came you to give Stellen-jager to the Fraulein? You know she is not an expert!"

"*Besser als zahlen auf,*" Hansi grunted drily, and launched into excuses: he'd thought the horse manageable . . . Emperor and Falstaff were men's horses, too big for the Fraulein to handle . . . Prince Rupert had tired Zinnober this morning before he left for Mainz, and Cronus had lost a shoe, with no time to replace it . . .

I stood, politely blank and suppressing my feeling of momentary triumph. But there was still plenty of doubt and uncertainty. Kaspar was inclined to go into a tirade in support of The Story, but aside from Hansi's one unguarded comment, I wasn't picking up anything helpful. "Do stop, Kaspar! I can't understand a word, but I know you're being unpleasant to Hansi, and I won't have him blamed. If anything," I said, sweetly, "you set the horse off. He was perfectly all right . . . until you scraped him with your spur."

There was a faint pause, which I ignored even more sweetly, giving the horse another lump of sugar and tossing the reins to Hansi. "I'm for a bath and change —coming, Kaspar? Good night, Hansi . . ."

Kaspar came to life long enough to say, "I must check Cronus's shoe . . ."

"See you at dinner, then." I went through the kitchen door, ran up the stone steps humming softly and feeling reasonably satisfied with a good day's work. *No result is still an end product*—so now I knew there was no innocent explanation for Nyx's disappearance—Kaspar and Hansi were in cahoots, and had tried to kill me. Now *they* knew I could handle horses, but I was still one up: they didn't know I understood German, and for as long as I could prevent suspicion, it was my ace in the hole.

Klara came beaming from one of the closets where she'd established an ironing board. "Fraulein, I never hear you sing before."

"Did you think I couldn't?"

She shook her head, tugging efficiently at my riding boots. "Not at all. Fraulein Nyx can do *anything*— that is well known from the films," she said. "It is only that I not hear you . . . but you save the voice for the work, *nicht wahr? Und so*, it was a good day, you enjoyed your ride?"

"Yes, Klara," I said after a moment, "it was a very good day, and the ride was—exceptional . . ."

Chapter VIII

KLARA DECREED I should wear one of Nyx's gowns—fashioned from a sari the color of creme de menthe, with a 12-inch border of gold embroidery and a swirling thin silk underskirt. It was a favorite, and Nyx had a particular *way* of wearing it: sinuous, bending, swaying like a leaf in the breeze. "It makes me feel like an oread!" she'd always said.

Evidently she'd often worn it at Stelleberg, for Klara had readied all the accessories of ornate gold necklace, evening sandals, gold-tipped pins and hair combs. I did her special eyes—Nyx had been using gold dust and sequins long before *Vogue* ever thought of it. I was so nervous that I was even fancier than usual, and emerged looking like a Rajah's Number One Girl, but Klara was breathless with admiration as she automatically handed over the bottle of Nuit de Noel.

In the long dressing mirror, the resemblance really was eerie. No wonder Kaspar had nearly fainted last night! I lit a cigarette and stared absently at the cheerful fire. I had him on the defensive—but he had Nyx, and so far I *didn't* have her knowledge. If I couldn't get her back before the elections, what did they mean to do with her?

I closed my eyes, sighing in frustration—and quite clearly Nyx's voice said, "I seem to have a dreadful cold, sis."

Sis? Meaning "disregard!"—but why tell me that? I stood shaking, clasping my hands tightly and mentally asking, "Where are you, where are you, *tell me!*" Once I felt a quiver, then it was gone . . . gone as completely as a broken telephone connection. I could still interpret the message. Nyx, from childhood, was always able to create a flush, a fever, to avoid something boring! Mother got onto it at once, of course, and instantly settled her hash by decreeing Nyx would miss the next treat. Naturally. A sick child must stay home in bed. If there weren't a projected treat, mother invented one.

That was how I came to spend my tenth Christmas in Hawaii. Nyx was left home in bed, with a trained nurse and without a Christmas tree.

After that, she did as she was told, but she never lost the trick. Occasionally, when all else failed, she'd say, "I'll give myself a cold." But why *now?*

"Because they're frightened, they meant to take her somewhere else," said my mind, "and she's prevented it by being ill, so they won't dare move her." It was a comforting thought: first, she must sense I was on the trail—and second, they didn't wish to take any chances on her death by pneumonia! *Most of all, I must be too close for comfort. . . .*

I heard the music as I opened the hall door; it was flooding about me on the landing: Ravel's *Scarbo*. It filled the hall, accompanied me down the stairs, swelling flawlessly from the great hall . . . and through the crack of the opened doors I could see the piano and *Rupert*.

The room was otherwise shadowed and empty. Alone at his keyboard, Prince von Aspern was absorbed—a brilliant working light caught the flash of competent hands, burnished the dull gold hair, and I stood enthralled. This one thing Nyx had failed to mention in her letters—probably because she'd long since given up the ghost on music. "Aside from Chopsticks, all I can recognize is the National Anthem—but only because everybody stands up . . ."

I dubbed her whistling or humming for the films. I'd always thought her tone-deafness responsible for her inability to speak any foreign language: Nyx couldn't reproduce what she heard. With English it didn't matter, because of her naturally fluid voice—but I'd often wondered if she had any idea how delectable she sounded.

"It's a pity," she said once, when I was dubbing the French version of one of her films, "but if I had your ears together with my eyes and art fingers, I'd be insufferable!"

Leaning in the shadows, watching Rupert, I wondered if he *knew* this. Klara didn't. Would Nyx have admitted her weakness so quickly to a new acquaintance? *Most* unlikely! She did things for effect, but only *honest* effects. Ask a direct question and she gave an honest answer—but she was incredibly adept at avoiding the direct question!

I went into the hall as Rupert finished the final trailing notes, clapping my hands softly. "Bravo!"

He looked up quickly, his smile suddenly fixed as I walked toward him. He stood up, closing the piano. "Nyx, you are always more beautiful, my dear—how do you manage this?"

"You're not going to stop," I protested involuntarily, as he reached to the lamp. "Please, no—something more?"

He withdrew his hand slowly. "Do you really wish it? Are you thinking you must atone for my bad humor the other night? Not necessary, darling, I assure you."

"I'm so glad, I don't like you to be provoked with me," I murmured wistfully, "but I'd really like you to play. Please?"

"Very well, what is your preference?"

"Silly, you know I'm musically illiterate—I like rhythm and a pretty tune," I sank into a chair outside the ring of lamplight. "Play anything, darling—whatever you like, so I'll know I'm truly forgiven."

He looked at me inscrutably for a moment, then he sat down and began *Liebesvalser*. Clever of him; I'd asked for rhythm and tune . . . I leaned back, completely abandoned to the delicacy of touch, sensitive phrasing, until he sat silently, massaging his hands. "Oh, is that the end?" I sat up ingenuously. "It was beautiful, darling."

"I'm glad you liked it. I had the impression you didn't care for Brahms."

"Was *that* Brahms? Well, I can't abide those dreary orchestral things, but maybe if you play to me long enough, I could learn to like a few things."

Rupert laughed heartily. "How about this?" We were off on a spree of Debussy, Faurè, Ravel. He was midway through Gymnopedie when Princess Adelheid came quietly into the room, with Lise behind her, carrying the embroidery bag. Her Highness checked for an instant at sight of me, put a "shhh" finger to her lips and settled into the fireside chair. Shortly, Wilhelm brought the bar tray, set another log on the fire, and still Rupert played, while Wilhelm silently distributed drinks: sherry for the Princess, scotch for me, brandy deftly set on the piano near Prince Rupert.

When he'd finished the Satie, his mother's voice said, "Prophet Bird, please," and we continued to sit silent in the firelight while a prince played for us most exquisitely. At last, he closed the piano, switched off the light, stood up holding his drink and smiling. "No man ever had a more appreciative audience." He reached to pull me gently to my feet.

"No audience ever had a better teacher!" We went arm in arm, across the soft rugs toward Princess Adelheid.

"Stand still!" she commanded, cocking her head to one side and contemplatively sipping her sherry while we paused obediently. "You make a most harmonious design, my dears," she remarked, "and now that I have admired you—sit down. Nyx, my child, do I dare hope you may yet learn to care for our music?"

Rupert towered over us, leaning lazily against the

mantel. "She made a valiant effort, Mother," he chuckled. "Imagine—she endured a full thirty minutes of French moderns without a breath of complaint!"

"Ah? Perhaps she enjoyed it."

Be careful, Mother's voice said softly . . . "No, I did *not*," I said sadly. "It was simply a jumble—but I am determined to be *good*, and not *look* bored or make Rupert stop his concerts for you."

"We must send you to Rome more often if it works such a praiseworthy change," Rupert teased, as Kaspar came forward with August bowing respectfully behind him.

"Herr Hogarth wishes to speak with the Fraulein."

"Heavens, is it *seven* already? We agreed on seven each night for a daily check on progress of the film . . ." I said to the Princess. "Will you excuse me?"

"Certainly, my dear."

I sprang to my feet, and met Rupert's eyes. He said nothing, but I felt waves of pure *rage*, mingled with hurt—as though he understood and bitterly condemned, and was concealing humiliation and restraining himself by main force from violence . . . He drained his glass, while I hesitated, half frightened, and said evenly, "Don't keep him waiting, Nyx." He turned away indifferently, to fix a fresh drink. "Kaspar, how did your day go?"

"Flip?"

"Yes. You're okay?"

"Yes. Listen, Hansi is the estate steward, up to his

eyeballs in whatever's going on—and I heard from Nyx . . ."

"What?"

"Shhh!" I was alone in my bedroom, and I'm *positive I heard her say 'I seem to have a bad cold, sis,'* get it?"

"Meaning 'not true'," he reflected, "but why would she give herself a cold?"

"I thought *perhaps* to prevent their moving her farther away—which would mean we're closing in."

"Logical deduction," he said hopefully. "God, I hope you're right! I haven't much: Hansi—you've already placed him . . . One thing: Robinson's dug out that Vogel was a Hitler *jugend*. I don't know how that fits, but Robinson's on the ball. Nyx is his dream girl, he's seeing himself as a knight in shining armor. Whenever we get her back, she'll have to pay off with a full-scale date."

"Your problem, not mine—and worth it, I'd say. Is that all?"

"All that's definite, but there's something . . . Forster's jumpy as hell, even snapping at his wife," Flip said incredulously. "Nancy's ready to break down and tell me what she knows, but he's still *official*. Should I break first, d'you think? Tell him our end, and maybe he'll trade a few missing pieces?"

"Wait another day," I decided slowly. "I might turn up something, or hear from her again . . . get a solid lead. Pry what you can out of Forster or his wife, and call tomorrow, same time . . . okay?"

"Yes, take care, sweetie . . ."

"Did you have a happy day, Nyx?"

"Of course. Don't I always, at Stelleberg?"

"You have an infinite capacity for amusing yourself," Her Highness smiled, "but while you were riding with Kaspar, *I* was continuing my embroidery. I do not mean to be overtaken!"

"You *rode* today? I thought Cronus had cast a shoe?"

"Yes, but all to the good, Rupert. Hansi gave me Stellen-jager, and it was love at first sight!"

"*Stellen-jager?*" Rupert's eyes blazed, whirling to Kaspar. "What were you thinking of? A horse not out of the stables in more than a week, and only fit for a man! You know Nyx is no stunt rider . . ."

Kaspar's gray eyes regarded me thoughtfully. "Well, as to that—oh, Hansi's mistake, of course; he's had the horse out, thought him safe enough—but I suspect our darling Nyx has been deceiving us, Rupert." He laughed lightly. "From the way she was leaping hedges and dashing around the fields, Stellen-jager was child's play, eh, Nyx?"

"Oh, bother!" I said with mock crossness and giggled helplessly. "So I'm indolent. I prefer a nice steady old beast to a skittish youngster—but that doesn't mean I can't handle high spirits."

Rupert swallowed the last bite of schnitzel, wiped his mouth and laid aside the napkin. "I gather it was an exciting ride," he said evenly. "What, exactly, happened?"

"Why, nothing, darling. Stellen-jager wanted a run when he saw the fields, and I let him out. That's all."

"Kaspar?" Rupert's voice was deadly as honed

steel: if he couldn't get truth from me, he'd get it from his brother. Kaspar stiffened, his fingers crushing a crumb, but his light tenor voice was as frank and respectful as always.

"That *is* all. I admit I was worried for a moment, but when she took the hedge, I knew she was in control."

"And where were you?"

"With me," I chuckled, "except poor Klinge was totally bewildered . . . turning around and around, Kaspar trying to urge him forward while Stellenjager was zooming about like a dragon fly. Hilarious! Klinge didn't know where to begin."

Kaspar shot me a venomous glance for covering him. "Of course not," he said silkily. "He's never seen such equestrian pyrotechnics before. Wherever did you learn to ride, my dear?"

"On Uncle Randall's ranch when I was a child."

"How I should like to have been able to ride *properly*," Princess Adelheid sighed, "but always, for my generation, those dreadful side saddles! And I think you ride differently in Western America from even our modern styles, do you not, Nyx?"

At her gentle voice, Rupert closed his mouth over whatever he'd been about to say, while I agreed there were differences between Continental and Texas modes of riding. "How much I should like to see a real rodeo," she said yearningly. "One has seen those tricks with ropes, of course, but in a circus or on a stage, it is not the same."

"No, I'm afraid it isn't, but perhaps sometime I can borrow Uncle Randall's home movies of a roundup,"

I consoled. "They're entirely real, I promise, and very exciting."

"Well, if you're in such a Western mood, Nyx, perhaps you'll ride with me tomorrow?" Rupert asked, smiling, as we went in to the coffee tray. It was amazing how his mood switched from controlled fury to sunny good humor!

"Of course; what time?"

"May I send you a note with breakfast? My appointments aren't final." He set the demitasse cup on the tray. "Mother, forgive me? There are phone calls . . . Kaspar, where do you go tonight?"

"The final rehearsal for election day drill. Mother, you will excuse me? Nyx, goodnight." Kaspar bowed formally, and the brothers departed into the hall, leaving the great doors half shut.

Princess Adelheid and I sat over the tiny Sévres cups, gazing at the fire, absorbed in our individual thoughts, until Wilhelm came to remove the coffee service. She fitted a cigarette into her holder, smiled gracious thanks as he pottered forward to flick the lighter, and bent to pick up the embroidery bag while he retreated. "And now, my dear Nyx, you will tell me what really happened this afternoon," she said serenely.

I bent over Nyx's embroidery. "Oh, there was no danger, Rupert was only fussing."

"Yes, he was born responsible, and of course he has a personal concern for you," she stitched placidly, "but I was rated a notable horsewoman. my dear." The faded blue eyes lifted, caught mine compellingly. "Why did the horse bolt?"

Damn, she was in the same league with Mother and Daddy! "You promise to say nothing?"

She considered. "Yes, since no lasting harm was done."

"Then—Kaspar's horse was very close to mine, his spur accidentally brushed Stellen-jager, who was fresh. He only started to bolt; he was under control by the time we cleared the hedge, but still needing a run. I took him twice around the upper field. Apparently Klinge was unnerved—reared and threw Kaspar; he was just getting up as I came around the first time, and he'd caught up to me as I reached the wood path."

"Thank you, my dear," she returned to her needle-point, "and so, you think perhaps you may yet come to enjoy music from Rupert's performance?" she said smoothly.

"Frankly, I doubt it, Princess Adelheid," I mourned, searching for a strand of the next color, "but if I never really appreciate, it's not right he must abandon what gives him—and you—such pleasure. There has to be reciprocity between friends, don't you agree?"

"Yes," she said after a moment, "you are wise, my child."

Tonight's bouillon was flanked by thin-slivered tongue sandwiches. "Are you too tired to wait for Rupert?" she asked, anxiously. "It is my bedtime—but on a Saturday night, it is pleasant for a man to drink his soup with a beautiful woman." I sensed it was half a command.

"Of course I'll wait, I'm not at all tired, truly." I stood up. "Mayn't I take you to your room?" Lise was already coming forward, however, and in a few minutes I was alone by the fire. The copper pot steamed gently over its warmer; the sandwiches lay fresh and succulent beneath a damask napkin. I put another log on the fire and settled down contentedly over Nyx's embroidery. All that was lacking was soft music. I thought of Rupert's astonishing piano technique; if only I didn't have to be Nyx, what fun it would have been! From what I'd seen of his schedule, when had he time to practice? I suspected he relied on the hour before dinner, and possibly had abandoned it because it meant nothing to her. A pity . . .

"*Liebchen*," the deep voice whispered softly in my ear. Involuntarily, I jumped, jabbing my finger painfully with the embroidery needle. Rupert laughed, and before I could turn, he'd taken the needle, jabbed his own finger, and as a drop of red welled up, pressed it to mine. "Now—we are of one blood forever," he said, and kissed me.

"Really, darling, how dramatic can you be?" I scoffed lightly, licking my finger, while he stanched his on a handkerchief. "Blood vows over bouillon cups?"

He stood back, smiling, his eyes dancing like a boy. "Brandy, no bouillon tonight. Really, darling," he mimicked in a sultry falsetto, "how *dull* can you be?" He swung away to the decanters, with an absurd imitation of Nyx's toss of the head, laughing over his shoulder at me. Shortly he returned with a generous amount of brandy in a delicate crystal snifter, raising it in a toast. "Nyx: *die schonste konigen von meine herze.*"

I stared at him mutely, while he sipped, his eyes holding mine over the glass rim—and I felt a wave of tenderness, an almost tangible love like a single shining filament of a spider's web, stretching across the glowing ruby reds and sapphire blues of the Bokhara, reaching from Rupert at the fireplace to me in my armchair. Blindly, I looked away. How was it possible *I* should feel anything from Nyx's lover? *Nyx*—oh, God, he'd nearly caught me again!

"Very pretty and so you say," I remarked crossly, "but for all I understand of it, you may easily have put a hex on me." The thread was broken instantly. At random, I bent over the needlepoint. "Was it a good day for you? What have you been doing?"

"Nothing to interest you, my dear, but—yes, it was satisfactory. All seems ready for success in the elections. By the by, I spoke with your father," he said deliberately.

"*Daddy?* Why?"

"We meet Tuesday in Bonn, didn't you know?"

I shook my head. "Only that he would go to Bonn from Paris, not that he was to meet you. I *told* you: we erase anything concerning Daddy."

"Yes, so you did, but there's no longer need for such secrecy between you and me. Your father suggested I bring you with me. He sent his love, and a message." By Rupert's *very* casual tone, I was on guard at once. " 'Remember *toujours perdrix*.' "

Well, I knew exactly what Daddy meant, "You can have too much of a good thing." He'd never completely approved our doubling. Repeatedly, he'd warned us not to abuse or depend on the trick, or we'd grow careless and wind up in over our heads . . . one reason we'd always held it to a minimum. From long experience, we'd learned Daddy has a bad habit of being right.

He was never more right than this minute! I looked blankly at Rupert. "Wouldn't you think my own father could remember I'm the family illiterate?"

"Are you?"

"Oh, darling, isn't it obvious? I was only let graduate from high school on condition Daddy promised not to try to educate me," I protested. "I'm good for nothing but Hollywood."

Rupert polished off the brandy with a laugh, set the glass aside, leaning forward to inspect the petit-point. "Very pretty, now the design emerges," he approved —and gently took it away from me. "You mustn't strain your eyes," his hand drew me upward, "and it is not too chilly for us to admire the moonlight and take a few deep breaths of fresh air to make us sleep soundly. Come . . ."

We went out to the lower battlement that fell away sheer down the rock cliff to the river. The stones were worn smooth, extending across the mid-section of the great hall, and furnished with sun-lounges and flowered umbrellas, tables and wood-slat chairs.

I swished forward with Nyx's particular motions for this dress, bending to crush my cigarette, swaying back to lean between the merlons. Far below, I could see a boathouse, two sturdy stone moles, an efficient landing stage. I wondered whether Stelleberg pro-

121

duced crops or something shipped to market by water
—or perhaps was a regular stop for Rhine boats, with
a road leading direct to the village. Couldn't ask; Nyx
would know . . .

The view stretched miles in every direction. The
ancestral von Asperns had been incredibly shrewd in
self-preservation, choosing a site that was very nearly
impregnable. Even when thickly covered by medieval
forests, it would have been impossible for river
marauders to sneak up unnoticed. A single watch
guard could have handled this side of the castle,
leaving the main body to be concentrated landward at
the drawbridge.

Absorbed in the scene, I suddenly realized Rupert
was not beside me. "Rupert, where are you? Come
see, it's so lovely tonight." I swung around, leaning
against the crenel and caught my breath. In full
moonlight, he stood near the open French window—
and I knew I should love him till I died.

"One can see the moon any time, I prefer to look at
you," he said in a low voice. "Beloved . . ." He came
forward swiftly and pulled me into his arms, hun-
grily, almost roughly.

Toujours perdrix, Daddy had warned, and although in one sense I could never have too much of
Rupert's kisses, in another, I was so deep over my
head I was drowning—for if I were head over heels in
love with the man who loved my sister, deliberately
allowing him to make passionate love to me under the
impression I was Nyx, what would happen when he
found out?

Moon-madness, but it was literally impossible to

pretend coyness, reject him, when every nerve in my body tingled! If this was all I'd ever know of love, if I had never to see my sister and her husband again—because he'd never forgive the humiliation, not Rupert—these moments were still worth it. For the first time I understood the Little Mermaid who traded her tail for feet, *knowing* every step would be walking on knives.

I was clinging to him, kissing him back, murmuring throatily while he talked hoarsely between kisses, *"Meine herzegeliebste, du bist so sehr suss, ich liebe dich, meine schonste . . ."*

Heaven knows how long we were embracing—until suddenly he thrust me away with a groan. "Enough of the imposture," he said harshly. *"Du bist nicht Nyx, du bist Katie."* He flung away to the farther crenel, burying his head against his arms, while I sank into the nearest seat, totally stunned.

"Du kennst?"

"Naturlich!"

So it was I who would be forever humiliated. He'd known, and knowingly, had seen exactly how far Nyx's sister would go, thinking herself safe to steal the intimacy intended for Nyx. I shivered violently—because Nyx's sister might have gone even farther; it was he who had withdrawn. "How did you know?"

He shrugged, throwing up his head and staring down at the river. "Almost at once. Little things; the different perfume—I felt certain you understood German—most of all," he laughed mirthlessly, "d'you suppose your sister ever permitted me to kiss her as I kissed you that evening?

"Or that I ever attempted it?" Rupert glanced at me sardonically. "Always, she was entirely honest— or I thought so. She loves this *dum goss* Hogarth, she came here only to spur him by jealousy. Between Nyx and myself is companionship, no more."

He moved restlessly along to the next merlon, while I was torn between relief and a wry amusement that I'd been trapped by a kiss I hadn't dared refuse— and had patently enjoyed all too much. "I was confused at first," he said in a low voice. "Hogarth there —how could you not be Nyx? Even, I thought you might have some reason for allowing me to kiss you, but in the plane, I *knew*."

"Where did I slip up?" I asked after a moment.

He faced me, drawing a long breath. "You didn't know she had confided *everything*," he said quietly, "even minute details. So I know Katie loves music and water, is bored by paintings and mountains, speaks foreign languages easily. Nyx can cook, design dresses, draw freehand—but it is Katie who sews more evenly and *in whose bedroom hangs the family sampler* Nyx has suggested my mother shall copy with our family motifs.

"Nyx reads most, skis best; Katie is expert with sailboats, tennis, card games. It is Katie who rides like the wind, *who can handle any horse*, even an unbroken colt." He came toward me slowly. "Katie who has brains, education, versatility, who takes care of details while Nyx concentrates on career.

"Katie—who can be the perfect wife for a man whose work is public, endlessly demanding—who knows unerringly what to wear, what to say—who is as much two people as Nyx herself, the quintessence of aristocratic formality when required." He was looming over me now, while I sat transfixed and speechless. ". . . but for the right man, it is Katie who will tear her heart out and serve it on a silver platter.

"She tells me Katie is beautiful, not merely outside but inside, and Katie is the one I shall love." His hand jerked me up and into his arms again. "And God help me, she was right! *Wie kannst du mir betrugen?*" he demanded vehemently. "Why could you not say she wished to be alone with her lover, that you would take her place while she was gone? Or was it some sort of romantic test for me?"

"No, no," I said wildly. "It wasn't a test—I didn't know she'd ever mentioned me. Please, Rupert, I never meant to deceive you—at least . . ."

"What then? Where is she? Why do you come to pretend?"

"That's why," I said, distractedly, "because we don't know where she is. Oh, Rupert . . ."

Chapter IX

"*Nicht mit Hogarth?*"

I shook my head, burrowing against him, weeping from combined nerve strain and loving him so much. "*Nein, ihr kennt nicht*—that's why I came."

"Shhh, *liebchen*." He picked me up bodily and sat down, gently wiping away tears. "I have undoubtedly ruined those beautiful eyes," he joked softly. "Another way I knew: it is a lovely dress, you wear it elegantly, dear one—but it turns *your* eyes green! Come, sweetheart, be calm and tell me. You seriously say that Nyx has—vanished?"

I lay silent, distractedly thinking what to tell him. I'd no shred of real evidence for an accusation of Kaspar. Rupert drew out cigarettes, lighted them and gave one to me—and I still didn't know what to say. "Shall I help you a little?" he asked finally. "First, I am selfish, I must know my own fate. I have dared to think that perhaps you could love me. Am I right, or merely egotist?"

"I love you with all my heart," I whispered.

"Enough to marry me and live so far from home and family?"

"Of course," I said briskly. "I was only waiting to be asked, darling." We wasted a good fifteen minutes in the usual foolishness of kisses and rosy plans.

"Also, wir sind verloben, meine Katie?"

"Indeed we're engaged, *mein herz*," I assured him. "Oh, when I think how dreadfully I felt to be kissing you like mad, supposing *you* thought you were making love to Nyx! And then to find you knew all the time—I thought you were playing games with *me.*"

"Never," he said emphatically. "The first kiss—I confess treachery, but at once it was entirely real. Now: you have had enough time to think." His eyes crinkled wickedly. "We return to Nyx: why did she leave, where did she go, why send you to take her place, where is Hogarth, and why do you say you do not know where she is?"

"Because it is true. All we know is that she left Stelleberg, an effort was made to prove she was in Paris. Flip had a wire; it only confirmed what I already knew—that something had distressed her. Flip was unexpectedly called to New York—he's in Wiesbaden now; I was in Calabria. It was only in Naples that I got the card," I said slowly. "It was our private signal, so I knew something *had* happened; she'd started to send for me—but someone else mailed the card."

"I don't understand."

I drew a long breath. "This is one thing she would never have told you, darling, but if you're going to be

127

family, you'll have to know." I explained the peculiar Hume telepathy. "We can't talk to each other, like Mother and Daddy—at least, we never tried. Now, when it's important, I only get impressions."

"What do you think has happened?" he asked presently.

"When I *felt* trouble, I thought it might not be serious. Unfortunately, it's true I'd feel a blister on her heel, Rupert. Flip promised to keep trying the phone; in a few days my feeling was gone—but the *card* was 'emergency'," I said carefully. "In Rome I found Flip never actually spoke to her; he doesn't understand German well, by the messages he got he honestly thought she was still here—and I only felt trouble from the card, which was a week old."

"But why did *you* not telephone from Rome? You'd have understood August."

"The picture in *Figaro* and the wire to Flip—*then* I was really alarmed. I couldn't think what to do but pretend to be Nyx in Rome, throw a spanner in the works and play it by ear."

"Why didn't you tell me at once?"

"Daddy," I said baldly, "and I didn't know you from a hole in the ground, did I?" Rupert's eyes blazed with shock. "*Think*, darling! I learn Daddy's in Paris, that it's top secret—I learn you've known this all along . . . and it's from *your* castle Nyx has apparently disappeared!"

He was still a bit dry. "I wonder you had the courage to fly back with me."

"Don't be snappish with *me*, it will never get you anywhere," I remarked serenely. "Silly, I *knew* she was alive! Nyx never gets into scrapes, but she's a very public figure; a minor accident can be made to appear sensational—always to be avoided not only for Nyx but for Daddy. So perhaps it fitted to have a substitute Nyx, perhaps it was what she originally wanted."

"You thought—I was concerned in this?"

"Perhaps," I said simply. "You're hush-hush, too. Even when it seemed you thought I really was Nyx, it only meant you couldn't help."

"I see." Gently, Rupert rose to set me on my feet. In the moonlight his eyes were crystal pale. "You have not said how Kaspar is concerned. Did he try to make love to you today?" he remarked conversationally, and snorted at my reaction. "You see, *liebchen*, I fear that's it—and all my fault.

"Obvious, he was infatuated . . . once or twice I suspected, but she said nothing and I was too busy to probe," he sighed. "My brother is inclined to womanize, although generally he prefers barmaids," Rupert shrugged impersonally, "but putting two and two together: I'm afraid Nyx found his attentions distasteful to a point that she packed and left, rather than tell me. Does this seem likely, Katie?"

"Oh, entirely!" I agreed cordially. "Nyx never *fusses;* she merely removes herself quietly until peace is restored."

He nodded, brisk with relief. "That's it, then—he was pressing, disgusting to her—you felt her shock at the time. The card—was it dated?"

"Not the card itself."

"Klara probably found it, mailed it only meaning to be helpful," he decided. "You invented the farewell letter, of course—but equally of course Nyx would have written one and would probably have left it where you said. I expect Kaspar suppressed it; he wouldn't know what she might have said. He'd learn from August that Fraulein Hume left in a hired car and he'd cover as well as he could—pretend he'd known she was going to Paris. August wouldn't question it; he'd tell Klara, who told Mother."

But of course August only *heard* a car, and it was Klara who only thought *Paris*—and never August who spoke to Flip . . . Rupert threw an arm about me, drawing us to the center merlon and the moonlit river below. "But—where did she go?"

"She has quantities of friends," I shrugged comfortably, "and she's only three or four days from here, because I knew when she was calm again." I'd also known the initial terror had become anger and frustration . . . but let Rupert work out a feasible explanation, and he contented, until I could find Nyx.

"Why wouldn't she let you know?" he frowned.

"I expect she did, but as of May 21st, if she'd wired San Sebastian, it was undeliverable; if she wrote, it'll catch up with me next week; if she called Flip, she found he was in New York . . . and I'm bound to admit," I finished ruefully, "she's prone to feel if she's all right, we know it, and she loathes correspondence."

"The photograph in *Figaro*, the wire to Hogarth?"

"Kaspar—covering up?" I suggested reluctantly. "And of course he never expected I'd get into the act."

He nodded, and apparently abandoned Nyx. "Now what, *meine schatze?* What do we say?"

"Could you bear to continue the pretense a few days?"

"We'll never get away with it," he remarked drily. "One look at me and the world will know, *lammchen!*"

"Oh, me too!" I agreed sadly. "I love you so much, it's positively *depraved*." His response was most satisfactory, but despite a few deep breaths, his mind was still pulsing like a mercury memory chamber at IBM.

"So?"

"Would you terribly much mind," I asked in a very small voice, "pretending you've fallen in love with *Nyx?* I mean, it won't give your mother a spasm, will it?"

Rupert's lips twitched slightly. "No. She will be—*extremely* surprised," he murmured, "but why not tell her?"

"I'd like to wait till Tuesday, for Daddy's approval," I pleaded. By the glint in his eyes, I knew he didn't believe a word of it, but he said only, "Of course—but Mother will be hurt to have had no hint."

"Couldn't you *whisper* it's settled, pending Daddy?"

"Is Professor Hume unlikely to approve?"

"Heavens, no; he'll be glad to be rid of me," I said lightly, "but you do see it's a bit of a bind? It's so titillating, suddenly to say we're engaged and I'm not me, but my sister? No matter how unofficial, some servant will pass it along—and anything one says confidentially hits the papers tomorrow!"

"Still, families always know."

"Yes, I'll phone Mother while you tell Princess Adelheid," I agreed, "but until we hear from Nyx, I think *not* brothers and sisters or other relatives? It's only a few days, after all."

Rupert's face went grim and he strode away, pacing back and forth. I hoped he was fitting my evasions to the concept that Nyx had fled to avoid attempted rape by Kaspar. Whatever his conclusion, he decided to let me play it my way. "Very well, I hint to Mother and we let onlookers think as they please." I was about to throw myself into his arms, when I sensed movement—a shadow . . .

"Rupert, darling," I said in Nyx's voice, "I need a cigarette—and this dress was only meant for Bombay, could we go in, now?"

He swung about and almost before I'd finished speaking, he'd moved soundlessly the length of the stones and into the hall. I could hear him, "Wilhelm, you should be abed."

"A program of fine music, just ended," the old butler's voice confided placidly. "I thought to remove the tray, but perhaps you wish more bouillon?"

"Thank you, no. *Gute nacht, schlaf' wohl.*"

But it had not been Wilhelm I sensed. Lingering in the battlement shadows, I heard the old man pottering away, while Rupert came back to the French door—and behind him, half-hidden by his tall body, I distinctly saw Kaspar sliding from the darkness of the piano along the wall to the hall doors.

How long might he have been hidden in there, eaves-dropping?

In the bedroom, I considered the mantelpiece door and the locked door toward Kaspar's room. I could block it with armchairs, but once asleep, would I hear if they were pushed aside? To my relief, I found a latch-bolt on the panel, an ornate piece of carving, swinging loosely on a pivot and fitting into another bit of carving on the door. There was no way to tell if it could be raised from the outside, but I decided to take no chances; Nyx would have fastened it, Nyx had vanished. I tried wedging it with folded match packets, and with a sliver of firewood, and nothing held because of the carving. Finally, I removed the keys from my steel chain and patiently worked it under and around, locked it in place and reinforced with the armchair.

That left the locked door—opening *out* of my room! An armchair would be no barrier at all, but Necessity is the Mother, etc. I hunted out a barbaric costume bracelet of huge base metal links finished in gold, plus every leather belt in both wardrobes, and eventually I had a continuous loop buckled about the heavy bedpost through the bracelet over the door-handle.

After that I went to bed. In the darkness, I tried to reach Nyx, but there was nothing. I fell asleep thinking of my happiness. Was this how Nyx felt about Flip?

In the morning, the chair was faintly askew, and my bed had slid sideways about half an inch, but both chains had held, and they had not dared shift the bed far enough to be able to get a knife through the crack to slice the leather . . .

Very soberly, I disassembled the loop before ringing for breakfast. Some other device must be procured before tonight. All they couldn't determine with certainty would be whether or not I knew an attempt had been made.

On my tray was a note from Rupert, "We ride at 11, lunch at 1, take mother in the launch at 3—*immer auf will ich dich lieben, meine Katie!*" I should have flushed it down the john, of course, but it was my first love letter; I added it to the brocade pochette. "Tell Prince Rupert I'll be at the stables at eleven, please, Klara."

By 10:30 I was stealing down the main stairs. The library door was ajar, old August's back was turned, and *praises be!* there was a fantastic baronial key. I slipped in and turned it before picking up the phone. "Flip, no questions: I need twelve feet of steel link chain, any sort—two padlocks to fit, and about twelve inches of very fine steel chain, no thicker than a key ring but *strong*—and one padlock has to link both ends of the fine chain to a link of the other, can do?"

"I'll try," he said dazedly. "What gives?"

"Extra security. Don't worry—but do your best. Deliver it *only* into the personal hands of Klara, *nobody else!* Insist it's a surprise for Nyx, and that Klara must take it to the bedroom at once—and the later you deliver, the better, so there's no chance for servant gossip about a present . . . understand?"

"No," he said suspiciously. "You're not planning some sort of escape from the window, are you?"

"Of course not! I just don't want that package available for inspection. I'm riding at eleven with Rupert, lunch at one, we're all going on the river at three —so perhaps I won't be back until just time to dress for dinner," I said. "Have you got anything?"

"Rosa is Mrs. Johannes Vogelhaupt—which is like being Mrs. John Smith. There are thirty-one in the vicinity, all being checked out, but it takes time. Robinson says Vogel got leave to return for voting tomorrow. There was a nasty incident in a bierstube last night, practically shades of old Adolf . . . Forster's sent for reinforcements. He admits he expects trouble tomorrow. Dubois says your father's safely in Bonn, with Herr Doktor Frischmann . . ."

I'd heard nothing, no click, no breathing—but suddenly I knew the connection was open. "Flippy, tweetie-pie, darling," I crooned swiftly, "I must go —such lovely plans for today, I'm late as late—not another word, hon! Divine to talk to you, not that it isn't super-marvelous to be here, but people will talk German and you know how I can't understand anything but English?"

"And not always that! All right, Nyx, baby—have fun!" Thank heavens, he was quick on the uptake! He hung up; I broke the connection briskly . . . gently removed my forefinger and distinctly heard a phone replaced: an extension somewhere. Did Rupert know? The evasive telephone messages to Flip were instantly explained, of course. August knew by a flashing bulb when the phone was ringing, but only went to answer it following the third flash, indicating the library was empty.

The extension had to be where someone was nearly always at hand to pick it up before the fourth flash of August's bulb. Whoever it was must nearly have gone out of his mind at Flip's insistent calls! Very delicately I lifted the receiver again, caught guttural German, a man and woman: "You know what to do, take no chances . . ." "Yes, at once . . ." Then the phone was replaced.

I was tempted to phone Flip again, say, "Rosa has a phone . . ." It could only be she, somewhere, guarding Nyx . . . but the risk of being caught by the monitor? The library clock softly chimed the quarter hour. The police were checking thoroughly—and I was to meet Rupert. I had another puzzle piece unbeknownst to the enemy, but a repeat call to Flip would be highly suspicious—particularly if, aware again of the eavesdropper, I had nothing much to say . . . Soundlessly, I turned the key, swung open the door and faced Kaspar, turning toward me from the last step of the stairs.

His cold gray eyes flicked over me, absorbing my riding habit. "Good morning, you are up and about very early." He came forward swiftly, but already I was out and around him—waving to old August who'd turned at the sound of our voices. "It's only the early bird who has a chance to ride with Rupert," I shrugged. Kaspar's face tightened in fury, but observed by the porter, he had no choice but to let me pass. I felt decidedly shaky as I walked up the path to the stable.

There was no question that Kaspar had wanted to back me into the library—to do *what?* Knock me out until he could spirit me away? After the attempt to enter my room, and the scrap of conversation overheard on the phone, they were closing in on me. If I told Rupert *everything*, could I convince him? Might he not think first that I'd fooled Kaspar well enough to try rape for a second time—and meanwhile, what might they be doing to Nyx? Oh, Flip had been *right* that my pretense might only endanger her life!

The only ray of hope was that the phone talk confirmed she was still alive. I still felt they didn't *want* to kill her—but unquestionably, now, her fate depended on what I did or said today. I went slowly around the syringa bush and could see Rupert, leaning against a saddled horse, talking with Hansi.

Hansi! Good God, how dumb could I be? Hansi— nickname for Johannes, known to be assisting Kaspar . . . who'd deliberately tried to kill the impostor with a high-spirited horse, who certainly had the extension in the estate office. It couldn't have been Kaspar; he had been on the stairs just now.

Instinctively, I whirled back toward the castle. It was no matter if Hansi knew the phone was in use, since he couldn't leave Rupert. I was nearly to the rear door when it opened and Kaspar stepped out in riding kit, wreathed in smiles as he spied me. "Nyx, so I am not too late to join you—but where do you go?"

"For a hanky and sunglasses." But of course it was useless; he wasn't about to let me out of his sight. "Klara will bring them." In a twinkling he was leaning into the lower hall, giving pleasant commands to the servants.

"I'm not sure where I left the glasses . . ."

"No matter, there will be a pair at the stables." He had my arm in a steely grip. "But the sun is not very strong today; perhaps they will not be needed, after all."

Perforce, I let him lead me back to the stables, chatting inconsequentially. As we came over the rise, he released my arm—but I wouldn't permit it. I clung closely, stumbled slightly to brush against him, drew Rupert's attention with a cheery hail, "Hi, here we are," and smiled intimately at Kaspar. By the time we'd reached the yard, he was damp with nervous perspiration under Rupert's impassive gaze.

Hansi was bringing out a saddled horse, "Cronus has his shoe again, Fraulein." I looked at the poor beast and thought he was wickedly well named: he must have been *born* old enough to father the universe. How he and Nyx must have loved each other! But by the tilt of his head, I knew he was already uneasy over what I might expect of him today . . .

Behind me, Kaspar was humbly ingratiating. "This is a private assignation, Rupert, or I may come with you and Nyx?"

I caught Rupert's eye and nodded slightly. "Darling, not Cronus—I *promised* Stellen-jager . . ." Rapidly, I circled Hansi and went into the stables. "Where are you then?" From the farther stall I heard a whinny. "There's my laddie-buck," I crooned, taking a quick glance about. A wooden door stood ajar beyond the wall pegs holding saddles, but there was only time to glimpse a desk, files, the estate office, before Hansi was beside me.

My eyes travelled along the saddles, and widened at a genuine Western type. "Please—this one, Hansi . . ." I gave him no chance to say a word, but went back to the yard. "Why don't you take Cronus, Kaspar, since he's all saddled? We mustn't delay Rupert; he has so little time for exercise . . . oh, Klara, thank you!" as she puffed up with hanky and glasses.

"*Es mach's nicht,*" she beamed, bobbing to Rupert. "*Guten morgen, mein prinz.*" She stood aside, as Hansi brought Stellen-jager from the stables, watching admiringly while Rupert gave me a leg, vaulted into his own saddle, and called, "Kaspar, we'll go ahead to the fields." Then we were trotting off with an enthusiastic wave from Klara . . . leaving Kaspar the choice of riding Cronus to stay with us now, or waiting for a better horse we wouldn't outstrip later . . .

The instant we were out of sight, "*Noch liebst du mir?*" "*Immer auf, mein herz* . . . stand still, Stellen-jager, this is important."

"I hadn't counted on Kaspar," he said after a while, "but I suppose it's better not to appear too anxious to be alone."

"If we run him ragged, he won't be anxious to come again." We were nearing the fields; Stellen-jager was starting to prance a bit in anticipation, and as Zinnober caught the expectancy, Rupert threw back his head and shouted with laughter.

"All right, *liebchen.*"

"No more German!" I warned anxiously. "You mustn't slip, darling, please?"

Rupert's eyes were brilliantly blue, but he only nodded evenly and said, "Shall we, darling *Nyx*?" With a flick, he'd headed Zinnober for the hedge, and Stellen-jager was racing after him. Even though I started second, the two horses were springing together, tearing up to the far end of the field— wheeling and off for the return, just as Kaspar came cantering into the lower field. Subsequently, it became a sort of circus, and I'll admit both men could out-ride me, any day.

Their horses were responsive, trained to the flick of a finger, and helped by masculine weight and firm hands, where Stellen-jager was new to the game. He was a good horse, though; if the others could do it, he thought he could; he wanted to try. He nearly unseated me once when he reared, but my hand caught the pommel thong and we got down safe, if breathless —because he didn't want to lose me. There is no greater humiliation in the stables than for a respectable horse inadvertently to lose his chosen rider!

"Don't try to compete; I'm not heavy enough to hold you down, understand?" We trotted around the field sedately, while Kaspar and Rupert did some curvets and formal weaving in and out. Stellen-jager was agog to try, but obedient when I said, "*Later* . . . I'll teach you to caracole instead." He had it pat after six turns! As I took him back to the head of the field, I thought I heard a motor on the side road—then silence. The trees screened the field, and I saw nothing when I glanced that way. Imagination . . .

"Now—show off!" We swirled down the field, full tilt, without a foot wrong, and tore around in a wide swing along the outside—and again I thought I heard a car, while I told him confidentially, "Now we're going to do a real trick, something none of the others can do—leave it to me, you just *gallop!*"

Rupert and Kaspar were leaping the hedge into the upper field, Rupert's face anxious. I'd probably give him heart-failure, but I couldn't resist and the chestnut *deserved* a bit of pride in the stables!

I looped my wrist securely in the pommel thong, and it was supple and alive. Heaven send I could still do the old Indian trick! I waved cheerfully to Rupert and Kaspar pounding up the field . . . rose lightly in the stirrups and did an approximation of an Apache yell . . . freed one foot and abandoned myself to Stellen-jager, lying hidden along his body and patting his neck.

"Straight around, don't worry, I'm here!" He'd no idea what I was doing, but he balanced my weight automatically and flew down the field. For a moment he was troubled, wondering whether he was supposed to jump, and of course he *couldn't* with the imbalance, but I tugged the rein slightly and he romped along full speed past the hedge, while I could hear the others racing wildly to cut him off.

I took a firm grip, braced for my return to the saddle—and under his head I could see *the estate jeep bouncing along the side road*, heading hell for leather into the woods, with Hansi at the wheel . . . but there was no more than a faint haze of dust when I'd pulled into the saddle again. I was too occupied in the

141

mechanics of my maneuver to realize all the implications at once—except the memory that I'd *thought* I heard a motor, and that neither Kaspar nor Rupert, tearing across the field, presumably to my aid, could have seen the car.

Rupert reached me first, pulling up short as I grinned proudly, "Surprise!" By his expression, I knew I'd better not pull any more surprises without advance notice! "Sorry, darlings," I said penitently as Kaspar came up, "but what with you showing off so magnificently, Stellen-jager was feeling a bit left out —and I had the pommel thong, so I thought he ought to have something to talk about back at the stables."

"A Texas trick?" Kaspar asked, while Rupert was steadying his breathing.

"Apache—one of the cowboys taught me. It's for circle fighting," I explained blandly as Rupert silently leaned forward to turn the chestnut homeward. "When the pioneers drew the Conestogas into a circle, the Indians skirmished around the edges," I widened my eyes and lowered my voice dramatically, "always circling *in*—closer and closer, until they could fire under the horse's neck while his body protected them.

"Moving in for the kill," I murmured limpidly, twitching the reins from Rupert. "Couldn't we go into the woods to cool off?"

"Not today." I was *wild* to be following Hansi, but Rupert's voice was authoritative—and for all I knew Hansi was only going home for lunch. . . .

"All right then—one last jump!" We were off, with Rupert after me at once, and a last glorious run until we pulled in for a sedate trot from fields to stables. Kaspar was following very slowly and, I hoped, feeling unnerved . . . although it was not wise to needle him too obviously.

"I agree you are a superb horsewoman, but you will please not try such tricks again without first explaining," Rupert said quietly. It was a statement.

"Yes, darling."

"I never thought to find a woman to love—and now, I shall be terrified for the rest of my life, that I might lose you." He smiled at me ruefully, as we came into the stableyard. "Hansi?" There was only silence while Rupert swung me down to the flagstones. "Hansi?" Well, I knew the man couldn't be there, of course. I could hear Kaspar approaching; I slid quickly into the stables, calling "Hansi?" while I dashed for that rear door—to find it locked. I'd expected it, but I had to be sure. "What do we do with the horses?"

"Leave them hitched, he's probably gone for a look at one of the plantings," Rupert said casually. He strolled down the path with me, Kaspar following, and dogging my footsteps up the stairs, to part with a casual wave, "See you at lunch."

I let Klara pull off my boots and draw the bath while I undressed and slid into a robe, to reconnoiter five minutes later—*and Kaspar's door to the inner stairway was open.* Only a few inches, but enough to catch any hint of motion . . . I was half-elated by his suspicion, as confirming that I was too close for comfort—and equally desperate to reach Flip. I tried the main hall door—and caught the top of Rupert's head trotting downstairs with August hobbling afterward. Obviously, there was a phone call for him—so *that* was no good, and time was growing short.

I gave up, temporarily, and rushed through bath and dressing. Nyx's make-up always took so damn much time . . . Klara bustled about, removing riding clothes and cleaning the bath. "It was a good ride, Fraulein?"

"Excellent! Klara, I expect a package, late this afternoon . . . you will be here?" At her nod, "I don't know what it is, it's supposed to be a surprise—but please bring it up and leave it in the closet for me to open?"

"Of course, Fraulein." Her eyes sparkled. "A birthday?"

"No—but someone whispered there'd be a surprise . . ."

It was five minutes past the hour before I got downstairs, and Wilhelm was gently sounding the gong. Perhaps, after lunch . . .

I controlled my impatience over jellied consomme, cold beef and salad. Kaspar was now angry enough to dare a few sideswipes over Nyx's equestrian ability and mendacity in former days. "Oh, *darling*," I protested, "I never said I couldn't ride—only one rides differently with different people. Now Rupert is a man of *action*—but somehow, I always thought *you* preferred the leisurely walking under trees . . ."

There was an infinitesimal silence, while I neatly dissected a bit of beef without glancing at Kaspar. Then Rupert said, "We go in the launch at three, if that suits you, Mother?"

144

"Yes, indeed, I look forward to it."

"Kaspar, you will escort Mother, please."

"With pleasure, but I cannot take time to go with you, Rupert. You will excuse me? There's still a lot to do."

"Nonsense, you're not a drillmaster, Kaspar. It's not a review for the president, after all; whatever the boys do will be good enough. You will see that our mother is comfortably settled on the launch and accompany us for the afternoon." Rupert's tone admitted of no argument. He tossed his napkin aside and rose, bowing formally to Princess Adelheid, "I have your permission to retire?"

"Of course, my dear."

"Three o'clock, at the landing," he smiled, his eyes flicking over Kaspar—who scrambled awkwardly to his feet, while Prince von Aspern, Head of the Family, turned to the dining room door and paused briefly. "Hansi will prepare the boat and take the helm. Inform him, Kaspar." Then he was gone, while Kaspar was murmuring, "Yes, certainly . . ."

I gulped silently, finishing the dish of wild strawberries. If my future husband was accustomed to display such arrogance, we were in for *trouble*—because nobody tells an American woman anything. On the contrary, it would be I who would tell him . . . I stole a look at the others. Her Highness was serenely permitting Wilhelm to remove the dessert dish and refill her teacup—and Kaspar . . .

Kaspar was reseated, shoveling up his strawberries with a speed that argued he was simply cleaning the dish. His expression was nervous; he brushed aside Wilhelm's offer of tea with impatience. His fingers toyed uneasily with a spoon—and I suddenly realized Rupert's high-handedness would immobilize both Kaspar and Johannes Vogelhaupt for several hours of the afternoon—because of course it was Hansi who was married to Rosa.

Now I was *frantic* to get to the phone, to alert Flip —for Nyx was somewhere along that road through the woods. There could be no other solution. Why else would Kaspar ruthlessly drag me away? Why else was Hansi haring off at the exact moment when Rupert's back was turned? Only my Apache trick had enabled me to see him . . .

Sedately, Her Highness Princess Adelheid von Aspern moved from luncheon table into baronial hall, attended by her guest, Fraulein Hume, and her son, Prince Kaspar. "If you will permit, Mother—I must speak to Hansi . . ."

She was as regal as Rupert. Singing into her usual chair, she inclined her head slightly. "You are excused until half past two, *mein sohn*. It will take at least thirty minutes to transfer me to the boat landing." I looked involuntarily at the ormolu mantel clock: ten minutes to two—leaving Kaspar just forty minutes to get Hansi on the job.

With a bow, he went off to the estate intercom in the library. From my seat, I could see the door shut— swing open ten minutes later—Kaspar hastily darting up the main stairs. My chance. "Have I permission to be excused also, your Highness?"

146

"Certainly, my dear. In fact, if you will press the bell as you pass, I believe I shall allow Lise to help me freshen for this forthcoming treat . . ."

I finally slid into the library, locked the door and dashed for the phone.

It was dead.

Chapter X

I JIGGLED THE buttons, inspected the wiring, even cautiously leaned from the window—but there was no break anywhere. I'd used the phone at 10:30, Rupert had used it an hour ago . . . *now* it was out of order, following Kaspar's ten minutes. What had he done, I wondered: loosened a screw, a bit of wire? I could have *screamed* with fury, because there was no time left. I'd bet the extension was still working— but even if I could reach the stables, the office would be locked. To break it open by force would only put everything in the open, *with increased danger for Nyx.*

I went upstairs and wrote a note for Flip, "Johnny Highbird is in our stable," and when Klara answered my bell, breathless and still gulping her lunch, I said, "Forgive me, Klara, but this is the most important thing of all. When the package comes, you must give this note to the man who delivers it—but no one must know!"

"It iss for Herr Hogart'," she deduced instantly. "I take care of it." Apparently Nyx had told everyone in sight of her unrequited passion for Flip—which made Rupert's theory of unwelcome advances by Kaspar even more surprising. Could Kaspar be the only person who didn't know? No time to think now—Rupert was rapping at my door. "Ready, Nyx?"

Despite the beauty of the day and the presence of a half dozen guests to create a cloak of politeness, it was not a pleasant three hours. Hansi was grimly efficient in taking us up river to the landing of a modest castle, suitable for counts, where the owners waited to provide tea. "You recall Count von Nordlicht," Rupert told me carefully, "and here is your great admirer, Nyx—his grand-daughter Anny. Countess, delightful to see you . . ."

Bless him for helping me, but nerve-wracking all the same. Princess Adelheid was enjoying the visit with her old friends; Anny was about *fourteen* and attached herself to me like a limpet, breathing worshipful thanks for the autographed photo Nyx had sent her, "even, silver-framed—Gross-mutter says far too good for a schoolgirl . . ."

"But not half good enough for *my* picture," I returned with a twinkle that brought an attack of giggles.

The party seemed interminable; never did time pass so slowly—but finally we were home, separating to dress for dinner, and Klara indicated an immense package hidden under my evening gowns. I chuckled helplessly; Flip was far from stupid! He'd realized if there were a package, Klara would expect to know the contents. It was wrapped in gift paper and embellished with satin bows. The chains were fastened to the bot-

tom and padded to prevent any rattle. Above was a
five-pound box of chocolates, three recent novels—
obviously read, so probably stolen from Mrs. Forester.
Klara prattled admiringly of Flip's manly face and
form until I reminded her she was to say nothing—at
which, she eyed me shrewdly in the mirror, "*Ja, die
prinz kennt nicht*," she murmured.

"What?"

"I say nothing, Fraulein."

Neither Rupert nor Kaspar appeared at dinner.
"They send their excuses, but there is some difficulty
over these elections tomorrow," the Princess said
placidly, "and furthermore, it appears the telephone is
out of order. The boys have gone to the village,
where they can be in touch with matters.

"It is vexatious, but temporarily we are isolated.
That is the worst of a castle, although," she remarked
with sudden energy, "I must say that a castle, inconvenient as it may be, always *operates*, at least. So
many of these modern inventions lie down and die at
the most crucial moments."

But Flip would have my note, could be working on
it despite Kaspar . . . "Now you see that American
women are not really to be envied for the pushbutton
existence, Princess!"

"I confess that's occurred to me more than once,
since we installed the laundry machine, the dish-
washer and the rest," she reflected. "It is pleasant to
push a button, but if the button pushes back, what
then?"

"Inevitably—a repairman. They are the second

greatest industry in America," I told her, straight-faced.

She laughed heartily, pushing back her chair. "Shall we have our coffee? Now"—once we were comfortably settled before the fire—"continue to explain the American way of life, Nyx. One summons the repairman, who says . . . ?"

"That it will cost more than the machine is worth to fix it," I said promptly, "and honesty compels him to inform you it will be cheaper to replace than repair. He also adds that this is a disinterested opinion; there is nothing in it for him, as he does not sell machines."

"But naturally he knows where they may be purchased—a brother, perhaps?"

"Occasionally it's a cousin or his wife's brother-in-law, although he doesn't go into family relationships, of course."

She laughed again, and became serious. "Are you really so helpless, then?"

"Of course not! The first thing any American woman does to inoperative equipment is kick it—or pick it up and shake it—or turn it on its side. Don't laugh; it often works!"

"And if it does not?"

I shrugged. "Then we get a screwdriver. For instance," I said ingenuously, "this telephone—in America I should simply open up the instrument, take a look, and possibly find all that was needed is to tighten a screw."

She eyed me expressionlessly over the demitasse

cup. "Do you think you can?" she asked conversationally.

"I can try, if you permit?"

"By all means, my dear. Ring for Wilhelm . . ." When the butler came in, "Wilhelm, bring us some screwdrivers, if you please."

"*Screwdrivers?* Uh, very good, your Highness . . ." We sat silently, finishing coffee, until he returned anxiously with a selection, "If I knew the size . . . I trust these are satisfactory?"

"Entirely, thank you, Wilhelm," she said superbly. "You may remove the tray." When he'd gone, she gestured at the tools and rose. "What is that expression? 'Be my guest'?" Together we went to the library where she sank into the desk chair, and I turned to the wall box. The single center screw was the likeliest possibility . . . Her Highness leaned forward, deeply interested as I rapidly removed the metal shield. Two wires were hanging free. "Where does one *begin?*" she asked. "Are you sure it's safe, my

"Entirely safe," I said, realizing the extension must still be operating: there were two wires neatly in place—and two other screws slightly loose . . . a blue wire, a red wire . . . Color-keyed? I hooked the tiny metal connectors appropriately and tightened the screws.

"What are you doing now?"

"Fixing the phone, I hope. Would you lift the receiver?"

Wordlessly, she raised the instrument; we could both hear the dial tone. "My dear Nyx, how extremely clever of you! It's immensely comfortable to feel we are operating again—but oughtn't it to be tested?" she frowned slightly. "I feel certain one always calls an operator at once."

"Perhaps we should simply call anyone—Rupert, for instance? If he knew our phone was working again, he might prefer to come home."

She debated for a moment. "No, not Rupert. He will not like to be disturbed, only to be told the phone works—and it's not certain where he may be. We might have to make a number of calls, which would disturb him even more. Rupert does not like any appearance of feminine hysterics," she said, and with sudden inspiration, "Perhaps your friend Mr. Hogarth? And we will leave the news as a pleasant surprise for Rupert."

Why didn't she want Rupert to know at once? I picked up the phone and got through to Wiesbaden. "Flip? The phone was out of order for a while, this is 'testing one two three.' Is the connection clear?"

"Perfectly," he said bewildered but relieved. "What's going on? I've been calling constantly for over an hour—I could hear the phone ringing, but there was no answer—and now you say it was out of order?"

So the extension was working. "Only a loose wire in the wall box, and Her Highness and I decided to fix it."

"She's there with you?"

"Yes. Oh, it was perfectly simple, but we thought we ought to test. Rupert and Kaspar are somewhere in the village; the elections seem not to be going well."

"You're damn right! Forster's worried to death," Flip said grimly, "and whether you like it or now, I'm telling him the whole thing tonight, and don't argue! You got the box?"

"Yes. Well, it's wonderful you're liking Wiesbaden, Flippy, darling. Have you met any nice people?"

"Only policemen, and they're too busy tonight to do anything about Johnny Highbird," he snorted. "For God's sake, stay in the castle and draw up the bridge. This place is as jumpy as Mississippi before a Freedom Bus crosses the state line."

"Sounds like *fun*. Well, darling, while you kick up your heels, I shall sit by the fire and go blamelessly to bed at eleven—call me tomorrow. Good night, sweetie." I hung up and smiled at the Princess. "Isn't there someone you'd like to telephone?"

"Yes," she said, surprisingly, "if you will be kind enough to find the number for me, my dear. I should like to thank Anton von Nordlicht for his courtesy this afternoon . . ."

I left her sitting erectly before the desk, the phone held a dignified inch from her ear, and in about twenty minutes she came back to the hall, looking decidedly pale and sober—but she said only that the night seemed unexpectedly chilly for this time of year, and would I be kind enough to put another log on the fire.

Then we simply sat, for hours, sewing silently. Wilhelm produced the bouillon tray and sandwiches; Her Highness said, "Thank you, Wilhelm—do not wait to remove the tray tonight. His Highness and Prince Kaspar may be delayed many hours. *Gute nacht . . .*" Lise came, and was pleasantly dismissed to bed . . . and I could still not decide whether to unhitch the extension. There'd been no one monitoring when I fixed our phone; by now, the situation might have changed. To immobilize them would lead to immediate investigation—*and they still had Nyx.*

The ormolu clock said one, and despite bouillon and extra logs, Princess Adelheid's thin fingers trembled on the needle. On the pretext of needing cigarettes, I ran upstairs, found two sweaters and a pair of fuzzy slippers. She only smiled courteously while I wrapped the cashmere about her and firmly tucked her feet into the slippers and onto a fauteuil. I pulled the heavy draperies tightly across the long windows and stoked the fire until it roared.

She was alarmingly pale, but I coaxed her to drink another cup of bouillon, with gentle reminiscences of her young married life, of Anton von Nordlicht and his wife who were close friends . . . but the clock said two, and we were running out of wood. Finally, the soft voice died away. Princess Adelheid was asleep. I added the last logs to the fire, pulled the fire curtain. In the hall I could see August drowsing under the harsh bulb. It would be easier to get wood myself than to wake him.

I went up, two at a time, to shiver in the chill of my bedroom where the fire was long since dead, and discard evening clothes for warm slacks and sweater. There was no sign of any intruders, but I fastened the chains in place, anyway, pulled a blanket from the bed, locked the hall door behind me and went back to cover the Princess. I brought two armloads of wood from the guardroom, and she was still sleeping peacefully.

I thought I would wake her at three and ruthlessly take her up to bed—if I could only stay awake myself. Pinching myself, I walked back and forth, desperately worried. *Where was Rupert?* From Flip's communique, something was afoot. There was no question that the Princess had learned of it from Anton von Nordlicht. How many times had she waited beside the fire, years ago? In sleep, the lovely face was infinitely sad. She'd turned slightly, disarranging the blanket, one hand hanging over the chair arm, and chilly when I touched it.

As I started gently to tuck it beneath the blanket, her fingers curled over mine. "*Immer mischgunstig, immer der meuchelmorder,*" she muttered, "*er* will *prinz sein . . .*" I knelt down, murmuring, "Shhh, *wir sind in sicherheit, auch Rupert*, shhh." She sighed deeply and cuddled into the corner of the chair, but her hand still clung to mine, tightening when I tried to withdraw. There was nothing for it but to make myself as comfortable as possible on the floor beside her, while I considered her anguished words. It was certainly true that we were safe, as I'd told her—but *was Rupert?* "Always envious, always the assassin," she'd said, "he *will* be prince . . ."

So now I could guess what Nyx had somehow discovered, what made her dangerous—yet if Princess Adelheid knew it also, why had Nyx been abducted, yet left alive?

I woke to a warm hand grasping my shoulder, gazing fuzzily at Rupert's strained face bending over me. The Princess still held my hand, but in sleep, she'd turned to draw me against her, partly covered by the blanket. Gently, I released my hand and let Rupert pull me to my feet. "Thank God, you're all right—she wouldn't go to bed without knowing, but I think she was warm enough."

He nodded sombrely. "Too often she's had to wait alone, but tonight she had you to care for her, my good girl." He held me close for a moment.

"But you're safely home, it's all right now."

"No," his lips tightened grimly, "it is all wrong— but no matter. Can you stretch yourself enough to prepare her bedroom, or shall I wake Lise?"

"At four a.m.? Of course not!" There was nothing to do, in any case; Lise had left everything ready, even switched on the electric blanket to warm the bed. Rupert carried his mother into the room, and she half-woke for long enough to be satisfied by the sight of him, and let me undress her and tuck her between the sheets. Then she was asleep again.

Rupert came from his room, shrugging into a heavy jacket, just as I closed his mother's door. His eyes were sunken, his face gaunt with weariness. "I must return. I came only to be certain you were all right, since the phone was out of order."

"Not any more," I remembered. "Oh, I should have insisted! Your mother said *not*, a surprise when you got home—but we never thought you'd be so late. Oh, to drag you away, only to find us perfectly comfortable—forgive me . . ."

"Nothing to forgive, darling—but are you sure the phone is working?" He strode into the library.

"Yes, it was only a loose connection in the wall box. I tightened it; your mother even spoke to Count von Nordlicht."

"Ah? I wondered how Anton arrived so opportunely," he muttered, and without thinking, I said sleepily, "but there would always be the extension, we weren't really out of touch . . ." and snapped awake at Rupert's expression. "There is one, I saw the wires when I opened this box—didn't you know?"

He shook his head, and sat down. "Go away for a little, *liebchen*." I went back to the great hall, built up the fire, heated the bouillon and laced it with sherry. When finally he emerged, he said, "There isn't time."

"There isn't not-time; an army marches on its stomach."

Rupert hesitated, then he sank into a chair, sighing. "All so much worse than I knew," he muttered drearily. "What can it matter now? All is lost."

"Don't be too sure. Eat first, think later. Open wide!" I held the cup and literally spooned the contents into him, alternating with sandwiches. At last he sat back and lit a cigarette. "What else do you know that I do not, I wonder?"

"Flip says Colonel Forster sent for reinforcements yesterday, and there was a bierstube fracas last night. I expect you know, but reinforcements might be helpful?"

"Very! So they have expected trouble . . ."

"Can you say what's happening, exactly?" I asked timidly.

"Bribery, coercion, threats of violence." He shrugged. "Katie, to please me, you will try to make yourself comfortable on the chaise longue in Mother's room for the rest of the night? And lock the door, darling."

"Yes, of course I'll take care of her."

"See that you take care of yourself, also." He stood at the foot of the stairs until I'd locked myself into her room. Very faintly, I could hear his footsteps striding away. Then I unlocked the door and stole across to open my room. The barricade seemed undisturbed. I pulled pillow and quilt from the bed, rapidly bundled together riding clothes, found a warm bathrobe, and transferred everything to the Princess's room. I was about to crawl into a cocoon of covers when I woke up: there *must* be an inner staircase for this side of the castle!

The entrance was not in the fireplace, but was even easier to find than my door: an obvious section in the wood wall panelling beside the bed, with a key and a top bolt. I pulled it open and faced a similar door directly across a stone landing—Rupert's room. I nipped across, and sure enough, the door was open.

For no reason but automatic reflex (since Rupert wasn't there, nor likely to be), I went around through the hall and sealed his room, then came back to lock and bolt Princess Adelheid's door, pulling the chaise longue against it. It was after five, and the sky lightening, but after the night I'd put in, I wasn't minded to be roused by early sunlight.

I went to pull the draperies shut and I was observing the stables. They were faintly lit, and I sensed *movement*—only shadows in the gloom, but surely those were men, filing out of the building, lining up precisely, *silently raising their arms in the Nazi salute* to someone hidden by the syringa bush. Then they separated into neat groups of six, stepped forward and disappeared—but the clear air brought sound: one, two, three, four, *five* engines, started and dying away rapidly.

I stood still, my heart pounding. What to do? Whom to tell? If *only* I'd asked Rupert where he would be . . . Should I try for Flip? Wiesbaden was forty or fifty miles away; the trouble was *here*—nor did I know where those jeeps had gone.

Call Anton von Nordlicht—but he wouldn't be home, he was with Rupert . . . Wake August, perhaps he'd know . . . Or rouse the household; with the castle awake, the Princess would be safe enough—but the live-in servants were too elderly to carry a message quickly, and if I tried myself, I'd no idea which way to go . . .

Through tears of frustration, I saw two figures rounding the shrubbery, walking leisurely toward the castle—*Kaspar and Hansi*. They wore a uniform that seemed blue rather than the former Nazi brown—but there were still the vicious belts and guns. I drew back with a gulp. Thank God I hadn't tried for the phone! Why were they here, instead of leading the pack? Leaning against the hall door, I heard nothing; they'd use the inner stairs, of course.

Dimly, I thought I heard voices, a door opened, a pause and a retreat, voices again—rather high . . . they'd found Nyx's room impregnable. Now what?

After a long hiatus, there was a minute click behind me: Princess Adelheid's panel door shivered—but the top bolt held. I could hear a guttural oath, a rapid test of Rupert's door, then retreating steps, while I re-locked the panel and frantically sought for something to block the hall door against Hansi's burglar tools.

The poker? I slid it through the medievel iron loops of the key—wedged a side chair under the handle—set the fire tongs at my feet. I didn't know what use they'd be against a gun . . . but if I couldn't lever against Hansi's force, I *might* be able to whack his gun hand and get him in the groin before he could recover.

Kaspar's door opened again and steps strode to Rupert's door, knocking violently. "Rupert? You are needed! Open, please!" Then apparently Hansi turned the key and *they* discovered the empty room. "You see?" Kaspar's voice was falsetto with rage. "I told you, the girl is with him! He's bewitched, besotted—but she *knows* nothing, we only waste time here, when the polls open in half an hour."

"She's suspected, she's told him, he'll be on his guard."

"What of it?" Kaspar returned, impatiently. "Who expects faulty brakes in a car he's driven only an hour past? And if she is with him, we have them both . . . come on, Hansi!" Footsteps again, a door closed and locked—silence. Reconnoitering at the window, I saw them striding toward the stables, heard the purr of an engine. Were they *both* leaving? Yes! A sleek sports car was gently bumping over the bridle path, short-cutting up to the road by the fields, with two figures in the bucket seats. *Were they going to get Nyx?*

No—they turned along the lower end of the fields and vanished. I was half-sobbing with relief, but still wary. Had they left a guard to monitor the phone? Did I dare try the library phone? It was I they were hunting; the Princess would be safe—they hadn't even tried her hall door, and very shortly the servants would be awake to protect her. I climbed into riding clothes, standing by the window, but in fifteen minutes there was no sign of motion, no sound. It was 6:30, the polls were already open, and at any moment Rupert might be deliberately summoned—lured into using the car with faulty brakes.

I had to do whatever I could to save *him!* I was out of the room, down the stairs shaking August violently. "Wake up! *Where* is His Highness?"

"In the village hall, Fraulein," he said sleepily, surprised—obviously anyone should have known *that!*

I dialed the operator, holding my breath—listening for that telltale *lightening* of sound that meant the connection was opening, but either Kaspar and Hansi had felt secure enough to leave no guard—or the man was alseep. "I regret, the phone is busy . . ."

"It is a message from Her Highness, Princess Adelheid, for Prince Rupert." The operator was impressed, but in a moment she was back: a conversation to Bonn, not possible to interrupt. "If I tell you, could you keep trying? It is that something is wrong with the brakes of his car; he does now know—Her Highness only learns *now* that all was not repaired."

The girl caught her breath. "He might be *killed?* Leave it to me, Fraulein—if I do not reach him by phone, I send a messenger in person, it is only two squares . . ."

"Thank you, Her Highness will be relieved—and may I have Wiesbaden 6245 . . ." A sleepy female voice said in shaky German, "Herr Hogarth is not here, I do not know when he will return," and was about to hang up when I said, "*Nancy*—Mrs. Forster?"

"Yes?"

"Please wake up—it's emergency, this is Katie Hume."

She was an Army wife; she said, "I'm awake, what is it? Flip's with Ted, all hell is breaking loose—everyone alerted for duty, women and children barricaded in the houses."

"More or less the same here—except there's a plot to kill Prince Rupert, and thirty armed men left Stelleberg in five jeeps at five-thirty this morning, I don't know where they went. Kaspar and Hansi are the leaders; they left half an hour ago, went the other way past the fields."

"Got it," she said efficiently. "Anything else?"

"Only, *please* somehow tell Rupert not to use his car, they've fiddled the brakes."

For tuppence I'd have pillowed my head on the desk and gone to sleep—but there was still Nyx. I might be convinced she was somewhere along that road into the woods—but how far? There would be nothing gained if I lost myself trying to find her with no directions . . . why hadn't I asked Nancy Forster to send Flip in a car? Oh, *stupid!* I picked up the phone again, dialled for the operator—and a *mascu-*

line voice asked what number I wished! I hung up with a gulp. They'd already taken over the telephone exchange . . .

Desperately I cudgelled my brains for everything I'd ever heard about the Hitler standard operations: communications first, then divide and conquer—the more violence the better. Seven o'clock, and the castle was stirring. Opening the hall entrance, I could hear cheerful badinage below, the clink of dishes and cutlery. I went upstairs, rapidly opened Rupert's and the Princess's rooms—she was still sleeping. In my room, I removed the chains and thrust them into the packing box in the closet, then trotted down the stone stairs, and waved to the servants' *kaffeeklatsch*, the startled faces breaking into smiles, and went up the path to the stables.

There was only silence in the yard . . . and no guard left behind, for a sturdy steel bar stretched across the stable door, secured with an equally sturdy padlock! Unless they'd left a man locked in, the place was empty. I stole quietly around the stables, heard the horses stamping, whuffling gently, and found no other entrance. Presumably they'd felt so confident of capturing the telephone exchange, a monitor guard was not needed. Hansi had barred the stables and departed—because down a side path I could see garage doors yawning, the interior empty . . .

It would take a crowbar to prise off the stable lock, but somehow it must be done—for otherwise Stelleberg was truly isolated, immobilized and without telephones, with only a boat that could not be operated by a single person. Slowly I went back to the castle, and with every step I was madder than hops, until I was *boiling*, along the lines of "They can't do this to *me!*" I rang for Klara, walking back and forth in the room until she sidled through the panel door, bearing the breakfast tray. "*Guten morgen, Fraulein.*"

It was time for the showdown to begin. "*Guten morgen, Klara, Wie gehts?*" I gave her time to absorb it, grasping the tray and staring in surprise. "I'm sorry, Klara, but I'm not Nyx—I'm her sister Catherine—and I need your help." She set the tray on a table, still eyeing me—amazingly, almost satisfied.

"Already I know without knowing," she said, pouring my coffee and nodding proudly. "You are not quite so tall—the color of the nail polish is different—you take less time in the bath, more time at the make-up. I think I have forgotten while you are away—but now you tell me, I see that I knew."

"Now you see that you are a clever girl!"

She twisted a corner of her apron absently. "It is this trouble?" she asked squarely. "Rudi tells us there is a bombing, people are afraid to go to the voting stations."

"It is part of that, but more—*sehst du*, Klara, we are cut off," I said quietly. "No cars in the garage— the stables barred—and the telephone exchange controlled."

She lost some of the fresh country color in her cheeks, but she only straightened her shoulders more sturdily. "*Ja*, that is always first, my father tells me. They will have the cables and the radios, too, and blocks on the roads . . . but there is my bicycle, Fraulein," she said. "What is wanted?"

"A message to Prince Rupert. I told the operator, but now—perhaps she couldn't reach him before —and he *has* to know the brakes on his car are loose," I said desperately, "but I'm afraid for you, Klara. We've no idea what's going on."

She pursed her lips thoughtfully. "I am of the village, they will let me pass—and at home is Willi who knows cars. I tell him either fix these brakes or make it that the car does not start. If there is a guard, we slash the tires," she said calmly. "Leave the tray, Fraulein—I go at once . . ."

"Wait," I said. "First—tell me where does the road through the woods lead."

She paused, her hand on the panel door, and looked surprised. "Why—it goes directly through to Viern dorf, about twenty-five miles, but it is a very bad road, Fraulein. The logging carts, you understand . . . they sink, they make ruts." She shook her head, "For Vierndorf, one goes the other way, perhaps six miles longer, but better for the tires."

"Then there are no houses in the woods?"

"No," she shook her head wonderingly. "No one *lives* there, Fraulein—there is only the hostel for the woodcutters, that Hansi's mother keeps for a month or two in the fall."

"I see." And indeed I did see, my heart pounding with excitement. "It is far? It must be very lonely for her."

"She is used to it," Klara shrugged. "Until Hansi got the good new house in the village, Frau Elspeth had never lived but in the woods." She looked at me, uncertainly. "You will not ride so far, Fraulein? She will not be there, and in the woods, it is possible to be lost."

"Yes, I know. I was only curious. Go along—I shouldn't have delayed you."

Where would I find a crowbar? That lock must be gotten off the stables . . . There was a knock at the hall door. "Her Highness asks for you, Fraulein . . ."

She was regal, a fluffy marabou jacket tied under her chin, a padded bed-rest behind her—and her face exhausted but indomitable, eyeing my riding clothes. She waved Lise away. "Go and fuss in the servants' hall," she commanded imperiously. "I am tired of you! I have never slept better, nor felt more rested . . . go away until I ring!"

Perforce, the elderly maid curtsied, but her face was stubborn. She twiddled about, picking up this and moving that, while I walked to the window and covertly inspected the stables, which seemed still motionless and silent. "Lise," Her Highness said, *very* quietly.

"*Ja, ja.*" The maid scuttled for the panel door, her footsteps clumping faintly down the stone steps, while I smiled at Rupert's mother.

"It was a long night, but he came home—and I hope you don't mind, but I stuffed you into bed."

She eyed me austerely for a moment. "*Komm,*" she said softly, "*kuss mir, Catherine . . .*" She held out one hand, waggling the slender fingers seductively and chuckling at my face. "No, he did not tell me—and I am so amused, I do not tell him," she said, "But all the same, I know at once!"

"Oh, dear, I'm a total failure! I haven't fooled anybody for more than ten minutes—not even Klara."

She laughed, pulling me close to kiss my cheek heartily. "You will never fool anyone who loves you, my dear. You and Nyx are different as day from night, inside. Oh, a *dear* girl—if Rupert had fancied her I'd have been quite content in his happiness—but at once she told me you will be the right one.

"I was so *impatient* to see you," she smiled, "and at once I knew she was right. *Ach*, it will be so good to have a daughter at last! And where is she, the naughty minx—in Wiesbaden with this Flip, I suppose . . . and you are going riding?"

"Apparently *not*, the stables are padlocked," I shrugged, "and Hansi is with Kaspar. I suppose he didn't think anyone would be riding, but it's—disappointing."

"*Padlocked?*" she echoed, surprised. "How absurd! Really, there are times when Hansi exceeds his authority! Of course you must have your ride, my dear—bring me the dressing mirror from that chest . . ." It was a lovely thing, inlaid with nacre and rosewood, intricate as a medieval manuscript illumination despite faded colors. Her Highness flopped it casually on her knee, pressed something, and the back swung open . . . revealing a neat selection of keys, hanging from tacks and neatly labeled on small tags. Very efficient . . .

She sorted through the labels carefully, murmuring indistinguishably and shaking her head. "Here!" she said triumphantly, holding up a ring with half a dozen keys. "I don't know which opens the padlock, but these are the stable keys—and August or Rudi . . . even Wilhelm . . . can saddle for you."

It was that simple . . .

The padlock key was obvious. I went up the path and over the rise, down to the stables and had the thing open and removed in five minutes—no point to finding myself padlocked within . . .

The horses shifted, snuffling as I went through the dimness. Stellen-jagger was stamping with impatience. "Yes, we're going out; be quiet till I come back." I tried three keys before I had the office open, and eventually I found the phone: handset built into the back of the deep desk drawer. I'd brought a penknife and a pair of sharp scissors—ridiculous, but all I had. I opened some other drawers and found a much more efficient jackknife as well as a loaded pistol, which was heartening—and suddenly there was a faint *brrrr* and a light flashing over the door. Instinctively, I picked the phone out of the desk, and a male voice said relievedly, "Steffel, you are there! Any word?"

"*Nein,*" I growled indistinctly.

"Don't take it so hard," the voice jollied. "It's only three hours before Erich takes over and you can join the fun." I snorted and growled again, but apparently it satisfied. "Oh, you're always a sorehead! If there's no word, I'll get back to work." I replaced the phone thoughtfully: three hours . . .

Now was the time to immobilize the extension. I forced through shrubs and sliced the wire exactly where it dove into an iron pipe buried in the ground. I backed Stellen-jager out of his stall and saddled him, feeling reasonably confident—because it would be a while before they'd find the phone was cut. I replaced the steel bar, tucked the padlock into my riding jacket; to the casual glance, the stables still seemed *hors de combat.*.

"Now, we're off! No time to play; tomorrow we'll have a ball," I said, and we trotted briskly up to the field. The chestnut snorted, but he was no longer fresh and the one jump satisfied him for the moment. We were into the woods and for a mile or more the road was easy—but then it grew complicated. The woodsmen had thinned judiciously, and there were subsidiary wheel marks leading into the clearings . . . It was still possible to follow the main road, if one concentrated—but could I retreat swiftly enough, once I'd got Nyx? I pulled the horse to a sedate walk and broke every branch I could reach, as we went deeper and deeper into the forest—and just as I was ready to *scream* with nerves, I saw the house.

It was a peasant hut, with a second story added and modern conveniences: poles carried wires, smoke drifted from a chimney, and a cement slab to the rear indicated a cesspool. There was neither sound nor movement, but I could *feel* Nyx. Surely, they would not have left the house without a guard of some sort? I retreated into a thicket and pondered strategy.

Cut the phone wire first . . . It was easy to follow it away from the house a piece; evidently it was a bootleg job, for the wire wasn't taut like the power line above it, fastened to the top of the poles. Mounted on Stellen-jager, I could just reach to saw through it. Next, to disguise the resemblance. I retied my scarf babushka-fashion, hiding every scrap of hair, put on my dark glasses, and sat for a moment controlling the sudden shakes. It was now or never—but Mother had thought I could do it . . .

I trotted briskly to the front door of the hut, pounded imperiously. "Open!" At first there was no answer, but I sensed surreptitious motion, so I banged again and shouted, "Open *quickly!*" A quavering voice inquired, "Who is it?"

"From Prince Kaspar, make haste!" Finally, the door was unbarred and opened a crack. A timid old woman peered at me hesitantly, and I thrust open the door with a vicious kick of my riding boot that nearly knocked her down. "Why do you waste time? He wants a woman—bring her at once. Must I tell you the meaning of the words?"

"Na, na," she muttered and scuttled away, "I do not know if I can rouse her." It was an *age* before she was returning, ruthlessly tugging my sister, who swayed from side to side, her eyes half-closed. She was barefoot, clad in night clothes and bathrobe. "Do not hurt her," I said sharply.

"It is only the shot," the old woman apologized. "Rosa gave one this morning before she left—we did not know we should not. You will explain to His Highness?"

"Yes, he shall be told you have obeyed faithfully. Bring her forward, see if she can be got into the saddle." Somehow we managed it, and Nyx opened her eyes. "Katie?"

"Yes, hang onto me!" I said in English, and turned to see suspicion in the old woman's face. She was grabbing at the bridle, "Wait, she has no slippers, I will fetch them."

"There is no time, His Highness is waiting," and when she was still trying to cling to the horse, I raised my riding crop slightly. Instantly, she shrank back, trembling. "That's better. One must always *obey*, you know that!" I turned the chestnut and trotted rapidly back along the road until we were out of sight, then pulled to a stop. "Nyx, darling, try to come alive enough to hold onto me. It'll soon be over."

"Yes," she said thickly, "it's only that damned pentothal they gave me, be a'right in a while."

"Could you sit up a bit?" We finally got her astride before me, and lashed together with the cord of her bathrobe. "Are you all right?"

"Yes, but my bottom's cold," she said wistfully, and nearly fell off while we tucked the bathrobe under her, but finally we were headed for home. I looked anxiously for the broken branches, and found I needn't have bothered. The horse knew the way to the stables. Unerringly he brought us out to the fields, where he was *determined* on the short way over the hedge. As often as I headed him for the road, he snorted and threatened to buck, while Nyx sagged against me groggily.

I pleaded and cajoled, but it was useless; he was positive he could do it, and while we twittered back and forth, I heard a distant auto engine, which settled things at once. He made it with only the faintest stumble and an instant recover—which would teach him a lesson—but I never want to do that one again, with Nyx lurching sideways and threatening to unseat us both. Nearly to the stable yard, I reined in, and got her off the horse. She was a bit more awake. "We're back."

"Yes, wait here, sweetie, until I put the horse away. I'll come back for you, but stay out of sight."

There was no knowing whether they'd discovered the open stable, the dead phone. I brought Stellenjager into the yard as quietly as possible, half-expecting someone to challenge me and keeping my hand on the gun in my pocket—but the bar was still in place. Of course someone might be concealed in the office, while someone else had replaced the bar, but when I cautiously opened the stable door, there was no sign of life. Turning to pull it closed behind me, I could see a form wobbling toward the castle. Nyx hadn't waited, she was groggy and stumbling, but she was headed for the rear door by automatic reflex. I ran forward, my heart in my throat—if she were to be caught *again* .. . .

No one appeared, however, and she'd vanished into the kitchen entry. Should I go after her—or attempt to put the horse away? It was too late really to catch her; I'd have to chance she'd reach the room safely. If Klara were back, she'd look after her. I unsaddled and replaced Stellen-jager in his stall. "No time to rub down," I whispered, hugging him tightly and giving him two lumps of sugar. "Oh, you were such a good boy, thank you!"

Replacing the padlock, I wondered what had happened to Steffel—and what the relief man would say when he found no one to relieve! Warily I went into the kitchen entry, but apparently Nyx had been un-detected while the servants were occupied with luncheon. I could sense increased trouble, though. Wilhelm and Maria were sober-faced, frightened, saying no more than bare essentials. "Her Highness directed us to serve in your room, Fraulein."

"What has happened?"

Maria shook her head warningly. "I bring—go quickly!"

I fled up to the room, and found Nyx asleep on the bed. I shook her awake long enough to get her under the covers and disguise her presence by an opened traveling bag on the bed. Maria was too disturbed to notice, in any case. She set down the tray and spoke rapidly, "A man comes to repair the phone, Her Highness sends word all is in order, but he forces past August, insists it must be checked—and now it does not work at all, Fraulein . . ."

"He cut the wire," I nodded, "but there had been calls before he came?"

"Several, and the Princess spoke with friends."

"Klara?"

"She stays in the village, no one is allowed to leave," Maria whispered, "but Rudi knows back paths used by the poachers. He arrives just now, hides in the storerooms—but there is a mán at August's desk, Fraulein, and another patrolling the castle. They say they are sent by His Highness to protect the Prin-cess."

"Blue uniforms?" At her nod, "Where is the Prin-cess?"

174

"Locked into her room with Lise, but if she rings, a man comes with us. Wilhelm pretends to deliver iced tea—then I bring your lunch, so they do not know you are here."

"They asked for me?"

"A man says Prince Rupert sends him to bring you to the village. He *insists;* we show him the empty room, but he waits in the hall, orders we tell him the instant you return." Her voice was barely a thread. "We say only: you left, perhaps you take a walk."

"Good! You mustn't linger—do they *inspect* the trays? No? Then, try to slip this between the tea sandwiches, and tell Wilhelm to give her a *look*— something to draw her attention, so she searches, you understand?" I scribbled "All safe" on a scrap of paper, folded it into a tiny square. "I want her to know I'm here, she must be worrying." I smiled bracingly. "Cheer up, all will be well in the end, you'll see."

"It is too much like the old days," she muttered starkly, and went away, after cautiously listening for a full minute. The instant she'd gone, I got out the chains and fixed the barricade. There was nothing to be done with the hall door, but wedge a chair under the handle and hope for the best.

Slowly, I got undressed. Nyx was still out, but her pulse seemed all right—as much as I knew of such things. My eyelids were drooping, but I forced myself awake, staring blindly into space. Where was Rupert? Surely, I would *know* if he were dead? But suppose he was not dead but under restraint? I'd retrieved Nyx, but what good would it do if Kaspar's *coup* succeeded? If only I could reach Daddy—why hadn't I thought of him this morning, after I'd called Nancy Forster, when the phones were still open?

I couldn't hold back tears. Oh, stupid *stupid!* Everyone at Stelleberg knew, understood—only a stupid American girl still thought "it couldn't happen here," even while it was happening . . .

Chapter XI

It was six-thirty, and Klara was shaking me gently and Nyx was smiling at me from the dressing table. She was pitifully thin, still a bit disoriented, but gallant as always. "Katie, darling—*it's all over*, everyone safe, phones working," she said, staccato. "Im dying for the full story . . ."

"*Rupert?*"

"Willi removes something, the car does not start," Klara said proudly. "The bath is ready, Fraulein Katie."

"How did you get *in*? I though I locked up so carefully."

"I heard her knocking," Nyx shrugged. "Those *chains*—oh, you were a clever bunny, darling! She had to come round to the hall door, but she said everything was safe, and Rupert called to open the door, so I did. Come on, I've had my bath, we'll talk while you soak . . ." She sat on the loo cover and continued her make-up, while I slithered into the tub and let the water wash over me.

"They didn't—hurt you, Meg-baby?"

"No, they were *very* careful." She looked at me over the hand mirror and said drily, "You really save me from a fate worse than death, darling. I was slated for Princess Kaspar . . ."

"But—*why?* What made abduction necessary?"

"I knew he was a nasty Nazi," she said, surprised, "and by my reaction, it was obvious I would Tell All as quickly as possible. So—they removed me."

"But *how* did you know?"

She shrugged. "It was—borne in on me. If I'd understood German, I'd have realized more quickly—but on the surface, all the phys ed drills and planned play for potential juvenile delinquents seemed innocent. It wasn't healthy by American standards, perhaps—but Germans always have adored dressing up and parading about—and Rupert seemed to think it was a good way to keep the kids off the streets.

"I didn't see any more of Kaspar than I could help —I thought he was a creep." She began the shading of her right eye. "Amazing that Rupert would have such a brother! But we rode together when Rupert was busy—and one day the little twerp was trying to make love to me!" She wrinkled her nose in disgust and began on the other eye. "He'd realized I didn't love Rupert, and figured I was just wanting to marry a prince—in which case, any prince would do. I didn't like to tell Rupert, so I quietly kept out of the way.

"Then Sunday—Wilhelm puffed up saying Rupert was wanted on the phone, and off he went, leaving me with Kaspar. It was blood-chilling, Katie!" she said in a low voice. "He was holding my hand, trying to kiss me, literally *raving* . . . He could offer more than Rupert, make me the greatest first lady in the world, not only queen of his heart but of the earth.

"I thought he was insane, Katie," she shivered, closing her eyes in memory, "and I was alone with him! I played for time, of course, and finally he brought me back to the stables . . . and apparently I said the right things, because he 'respected me for my demands, but he was still the happiest man alive, for all would be demonstrated in two weeks.'

"I couldn't think *what* to do, I was so frightened. I got as far as writing you a card . . ."

"I got it, ten days later in Naples."

"You *got* it?"

"That's why I'm here. Go on," I crawled out, patted dry.

"Well, next day Rupert *swore* nothing would prevent our ride . . . I went to the stables—no one around, no horses waiting . . . I went in, the place was empty, the office open—dawdled around looking at the framed pix of their prize horses, and the one over the desk was crooked. You know how I can't *stand* that?

"So I straightened it—and behind it was a scale plan of election districts, marked with colored pins and names—all boys in Kaspar's drill club, Katie, and a tiny swastika in the corner! I nearly *died* . . . and then I heard a buzz in the drawer, so I pulled it open —and there was a phone, and when I picked it up, I could hear *Rupert* talking." She widened her eyes at me. "Well, it didn't take giant intellect to figure something was up."

"What then?"

"I put the phone back and got the hell out, natch! I looked at the river, and all of a sudden Hansi turns up *behind* me, saying Prince von Aspern's apologies but he was unable to ride, after all—but I could tell Hansi *knew*."

"Of course. You *straightened* the picture, sweetie. . . ." I pulled on hose, underwear, shoes, while Klara was draping the sari dress on Nyx, "Go on."

"I was going to tell Rupert; I never got a chance. First we were at dinner, and later he went off with Kaspar—and I waited and waited, until Wilhelm came for the tray and said, didn't I know His Highness had flown to Bonn and wouldn't be back till next day? So I went to bed—and next thing I knew I was in a perfectly strange bedroom," she finished simply, "and it wasn't even next day, but *two* days later.

"I was in nightclothes, the door was locked, and it was pitch black outside, except I knew there were trees—obviously a forest, but I'd no idea *where*, Katie. There was an old woman who only spoke German, and a younger blonde who spoke English with a peculiar accent . . ."

"Rosa Martineau—Hansi's Alsacian wife."

"Oh? Well, she said I was only in 'protective custody' for my own safety, by His Highness's orders. I had a few words to say," she remarked, "but it did no good—and they were quite *kind*: not bad food, got me some English books and magazines, but the thing was: I hadn't the least *clue* to where I was, Katie, plus no proper clothes! I could hear a phone bell, but I never had a chance to reach it.

"Then a few days ago I *felt* you—and next night there was a hell of a flap downstairs, phone calls and loud angry male voices, but all German so I couldn't understand, and finally it calmed down and Rosa came up with hot chocolate before bedtime. I was dumb enough to drink it!" Nyx said disgustedly, "and next day I woke with a headache, and Rosa comes tootling in with a peasant blouse and skirt. She said we were going for a *lovely* drive . . . so I gave myself a cold, because I was *sure* you were on the trail."

"I heard you. Did you ever hear me?"

"Once I *thought* you said 'I'm coming,' but mostly I wasn't sure of my own name. Yesterday Rosa gave me an injection, supposed to be penicillin, but I overheard 'pentothal'—and apparently I got some more this morning. That's all. Then you came and got me." She finished her hair and moved away from the dressing table. "Now you—tell while I make you up."

"I was worried by the card, and I took your place —because it was meant to involve Daddy. He's in Bonn. Flip's in Wiesbaden, and Rupert and I are engaged."

"*Well*, that was fast work, sweetie!"

"*Procureuse!*"

"Not if you're *engaged*," she said austerely. "How's Flip?"

"Writing a proposal speech. I told him it was required."

"*Procureuse*, yourself!" She dimpled and began the other half of my face. "Go on."

181

"Too much to tell—Kaspar nearly fainted when he saw me, of course. That's when they wanted to re-*move you. The election upset began yesterday.* Kaspar put the phone out of order, but I fixed it with a screwdriver and we got a few messages through, before they cut the main line. I was certain you were in the woods, but the cars were gone and the stables were padlocked—except that Princess Adelheid had a duplicate key. So I came and got you. That's all—but is it really over? Where's Rupert?"

"Downstairs in a conclave," Nyx was dabbing me with her perfume, while Klara brushed my hair into the swirl, and fastened a mishmash of gold chains about my throat.

"Princess Adelheid?"

"How *peculiarly* you say it," Nyx remarked, while Klara grinned at me wickedly.

"Princess Addeli-eed is waiting in the hall," she said, giggling. Oh, dear, so *that* was how Rupert's mother had known! Nyx called her "Adelaide," four-square American . . .

"Oh well—" I stood up, surveying myself in the mirror, on fire to get downstairs and make sure with my own eyes that Rupert was all right . . . and Nyx was suddenly beside me. Silently her eyes met mine in the glass, and except for our dresses—hers green, mine blue—we were *twins*, from top to toe. We were even the same height: Nyx in low Oriental gold sandals—me in stiletto heels . . . her eyes less blue with green shadowing, mine less green with blue make-up and dress.

"For the last time, I think," she said reflectively, "so let's make it good?"

Quietly we went down the main stairs, matching our steps. There were six American GI's in the lower hall—bug-eyed when they spotted us, but aside from one lad who swallowed his chewing gum from surprise, we were not challenged. Near the bottom steps, Nyx caught my arm and we lurked, eavesdropping . . .

Rupert's voice: "Do you seriously tell me you were unaware that Vogelhaupt turned your boys' clubs into armed terrorists, Kaspar?"

"I knew *nothing*, Rupert!" Kaspar's voice was high, shaky, yet earnest and respectful as always. "How can you *ask*—when I have spent this day, like yourself, working shoulder to shouldeer with the authorities to control, avert bloodshed! In all these years since childhood in the Maquis, do I *deserve* these doubts, my brother?"

"I ask only that you dispel them."

"What more can I say? I repeat: I knew nothing of an extension telephone, nothing of a cache of arms, nothing of the special drills—only that occasionally, when you needed me elsewhere, Vogelhaupt took charge in my absence."

Nyx tugged my elbow and silently we went forward to the great hall that was obscured from us by a ring of large solid masculine backs, mostly in uniform. "*Nothing* of the wall plan in the estate office, showing election districts, marked with colored pins, names of your boys—*and a swastika?*" Nyx's voice projected over, around, through the room, as she poked me.

"*Nothing* of the thirty uniformed armed men whom you reviewed in the stableyard at five-thirty this morning, and dispatched in five jeeps before driving away yourself with Hansi?" I asked, using Nyx's voice.

Startled, the crowd parted before us, moving aside until we faced the group before the fireplace: Rupert, Kaspar, Princess Adelheid sitting aside in her chair, Count von Nordlicht behind her.

"*Nothing* of the faulty brakes on Prince von Aspern's car, today?" Nyx asked, deadly soft, pacing forward.

"*Nothing* of your promise to make Nyx queen of the earth, once elections were over?" I chorused.

"Nor the library telephone out of order only two minutes after you had used it?"

"The house in the woods—Rosa Martineau . . ."

Kaspar went to pieces at once, screaming like a cornered rabbit, "No, no—nothing, *nothing!*" and staring at us white-faced, while Nyx and I simply stood: side by side, expressionless.

Then Flip thrust frantically through the ring of officers, crying, "Nyx, baby!" We *both* looked at him. Rupert strode forward, "Katie, *liebchen!*" We both looked at *him*—until Flip had got Nyx into his arms and simultaneously Rupert was holding me.

There was a sudden scuffle, a shout, a concerted rush for the great windows to the battlement . . . two shots in rapid succession . . . Even as Rupert went, ashen and grim with control, I wondered why

I'd never realized there would be a direct entrance to the battlement, connecting with the inner stairs to the guardroom? In the dim light from the great hall, I could see Hansi, standing in the grip of an American officer, the gun arm hanging uselessly . . .

The Princess sat still, her chin firm with effort, while I knelt beside her. Her fingers trembled, but she simply *sat*, staring ahead, while there was a subdued bustle outside. Presently, Nyx came to kneel at the other side, and at long last, a few of the top brass walked quietly through the farther window with Rupert. Anton von Nordlicht and another man came across to bend in silent sympathy over the Princess's hand; the others merely bowed formally and filed out to the hall.

"Where is your man, my dear?" the Princess turned to Nyx.

Flip materialized from the farthest shadows. "Here —is there something I can do, your Highness?"

"No—except come into the light." Obediently Flip circled, hunched onto the fauteuil setting one arm around Nyx. Princess Adelheid surveyed him carefully. "Yes, you will be most suitable," she stated, "and your first task will be to prepare a drink for me. Brandy with a little soda, please."

"With pleasure," Flip said softly, drawing Nyx with him to the bar tray, while the Princess drew a little sighing breath, and sat up even more squarely.

"So—it is over," she murmured in German. "You— know, don't you, Katie?"

"Yes." Only truth would suffice now. "That is—I suspected."

"I, too—there is no proof, but I *know*." She shrugged. "Who knows why, in a field of sweet corn, one ear of a stalk has ergot? Or families, also."

"Shhh, think instead that the best has remained . . ."

"Yes, but Charles and Dieter . . . *hard* to lose two for one." Her fingers clenched my hand cruelly, anguished, then released me, as Flip brought the drinks, one for each of us. He cleared his throat diffidently, standing on the Bokhara before the fireplace and raising his glass.

"To the House of Aspern . . ."

Princess Adelheid looked intently at her glass while we drank the toast. "I shall drink, too," she announced. "We have survived eight hundred years. I expect we'll—survive this day, also." She emptied her glass, set it aside and rose. "I shall not wait for Rupert. If you will forgive me, I shall retire. It has been a . . . long day . . ."

Nor was it over. By tacit agreement, we had pulled the draperies across the battlement windows before we ate a tasteless dinner, served by Wilhelm, sober-faced and taut with control. American GI's still guarded the castle, as well as the airstrip and the stables, on the bare chance some of the gang might try escape on horseback. Rupert was still at the village hall. Flip stayed within reach of the phone, while Nyx and I talked disjointedly in the great hall.

He came in finally to report a phone call from Robinson, who'd been quick enough to inform the German Embassy about Vogel, whereby they'd dug around and turned up a couple of other new Nazis. "Vogel is Hansi's kid brother; we might have guessed that. They got him and Rosa at the house in the woods. The old mother doesn't know anything, but Rosa admits Hansi meant to use Nyx to pressure Professor Hume into cooperating with the new regime. From the extension phone, they knew he was in Paris at the Merciers; Rupert talked to him there.

"They knew there was a sister Katie; they *didn't* know the resemblance, so the Rome airport pictures knocked 'em for a loop, especially as they'd just set up the Paris deal. Hansi phoned the brother to find out who you were, and got Rosa out of Paris. When you showed up here, they didn't know *what* to think, except that it was some deep dark plan of Rupert's. Then Kaspar overheard enough to realize you were Katie and understood German, and after that . . ." Flip shrugged, uncomfortably.

"They had to get me as well as Rupert," I finished.

Flip nodded grimly. "Forster says they've rounded up all but two. Now they're deciding whether to scrap these results and hold a new election."

By midnight it was settled that the votes were sufficiently reliable; Rupert's party had still won handsomely over the legitimate opposition, and Hansi's coup had failed.

"Only because you thought of telling Mrs. Forster," Rupert sank into a chair wearily. "She'd already alerted everybody before they could reach the Wiesbaden phones. We didn't know where or how they meant to strike, but we were prepared. It was a good plan. If we'd been caught unawares, likely it would have succeeded—which is a frightening thought."

"Yes, but it didn't happen, darling."

"Only because of two smart American girls and the American Army," he muttered, bitterly. "Oh, what was I thinking of, Katie! Of all people, I should have known. Kaspar always followed Hansi's lead; the twins and I were older, too grand to be playmates. Kaspar grew up with the stableboy." He sighed. "The Vogelhaupts were respectable, a part of Stelleberg from the great-grandfather. But for the war, Kaspar would have gone away to school, and the tie would have loosened. Instead—Father died. I was head of the family when I was a college boy. When the Nazis pressed—we packed and left.

"Afterwards—I knew Hansi had been in the German Army, but he convinced me he was never a Nazi, he fought only because he had no choice, and Katie, that *is* true for some men." Rupert's lips twisted sadly. "He was immensely clever, and Kaspar was completely under his thumb . . . but recently, once or twice, I was surprised by a minor leak, once or twice there were—accidents that were almost too fortuitous.

"Like Charles and Dieter," he said in a low voice. "It could only have been Kaspar. How could I have refused to admit this; why couldn't I have watched more carefully, been less trusting!"

"Because you were busy, and Hansi took pains to convince you Kaspar had matured."

"I should not have been so busy. Now—there are a dozen houses bombed, a hundred people physically

hurt, five hundred who are *afraid*—remembering
. . . And Kaspar is dead."

"Better so," I said after a moment. "There is no
way to freshen the rotten egg, darling." He nodded
silently, turning to pillow his head against my
shoulder. In a split second he was asleep. Nyx came
into the hall, Flip beside her, both of them walking
softly at my imperative gestture of *Shhhhh!*—but
Rupert never woke when they lifted his long legs onto
the fauteuil. Flip built up the fire, Nyx stuffed a pillow
under my back and a cigarette into my mouth. We
whispered over a final nightcap, and Rupert never
stirred.

"There's an awful lot of him, Katie. If we have a
double ceremony, he'll dwarf everybody."

"We aren't going to have a double ceremony," I
was firm. "I don't care if he dwarfs me, but I'm taking
no chances on finding the minister's married him to
you by mistake."

"Or Katie to me!" Flip's voice was horrified.

We suppressed giggles. "*When?*"

Daddy says the American Embassy in Bonn for us,
end of the week; he thought probably here for you,"
Nyx whispered. "Then he asked Mother, and called
back to deliver The Word." Nyx widened her eyes
blandly. "Mother says *he's* good enough for me, but
you have to have *her*; she's already ordered your dress
from Don Loper; it'll be ready Friday. She's got res-
ervations for Sunday, and a hat is all right for a film
star, but she's bringing great-grandmother's veil for
you . . .

"As well as Georgie and Sylvia," Nyx finished,

waggling her eyebrows wickedly. "She thinks it'll be very *educational* for them to see a feudal wedding."

"Is *that* what I am going to have?"

"If Mother says so—you are," Nyx shrugged, "but if it means riding side saddle on a white donkey, rather you than I!" That time I nearly broke apart, and Rupert shifted against my quivering shoulder with a deep sigh.

"*Quit* making me laugh, he's half dead, poor baby . . ."

"Baby?" Flip protested. "The size of him!"

"Yes—I'm not sure it's safe to let you marry him, sweetie," Nyx agreed, "unless he sleeps *very* quietly —because if he ever rolls over in the night, you'll be pancakes for breakfast."

"Not fair," I said indignantly. "I'm not snide about your choice! What else about Daddy?"

"He was a big *austere*. He hopes this will teach us a lesson," she admitted, "but then he broke down. Mother means to travel with Georgie and Sylvia all summer—and send them home alone, because she thinks it's more economical just to *stay* here until Daddy's officially notified about the Nobel Prize."

"At Stelleberg! Won't she and Princess Adelheid adore each other."

"I expect so . . . but Daddy says," Nyx looked at me very seriously, "when he gets it, he'll accept for you, too—because apparently this was awfully dangerous. If you hadn't blitzed the Stelleberg operation, there were to be uprisings all over.

"He said to tell you he is proud you are his daughter."

"Stop looking pathetic, darling," I murmured, unimpressed. "You got what you wanted; I've got what I want—what more could anyone ask?"

"Only the dawn of a new day," Rupert said deeply. "Pull back the draperies, Hogarth, so we may all begin together . . ."

IMPORTANT! To receive free advance news of exciting new LANCER BOOKS each month send your name and address to:

LANCER BOOKS, INC. • Dept. PDC-L
185 Madison Avenue • New York 16, New York

FROM LANCER
AN EXCITING LINE
OF GOTHIC-ROMANCE MYSTERIES

EVIL IN THE HOUSE by Evelyn Bond 72-908 (50¢). The ancient curse on the old New England mansion threatens a young boy's sanity and a woman's life.

DAY OF THE ARROW by Philip Loraine 72-909 (50¢). In their ancestral castle, a young Frenchwoman furtively seeks the cause of the half-seen forces which haunt her husband. This book will soon be a major motion picture.

NIGHTMARE IN JULY by Clara Coleman 72-911 (50¢). Amanda Swanson sensed a terrifying evil in the stranger's cold blue eyes . . . a life-threatening evil which followed her from the city's canyons to an old house hidden deep in the country.

CLOUDS OVER VELLANTI by Elsie Lee 72-919 (50¢). Inexorably, the innocent Megan Royce was drawn into the whirlwind of mysterious forces that buffeted the old Italian castle.

THE BROODING HOUSE by Alice Brennan 72-920 (50¢). It was not only her patient's approaching death which frightened the young nurse—It was the menace and terror she felt in every corner of this sinister house.

THE HOUSE ON THE FENS by Catherine Marchant 73-443 (60¢). Rosamund Morley was magnetically drawn to the man they called, *The Fen Tiger*. A frightening man whose past was shadowed and whose future led to unavoidable tragedy.

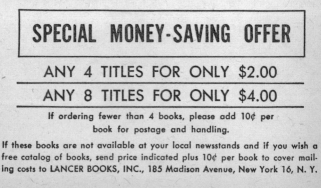

SPECIAL MONEY-SAVING OFFER

ANY 4 TITLES FOR ONLY $2.00
ANY 8 TITLES FOR ONLY $4.00

If ordering fewer than 4 books, please add 10¢ per book for postage and handling.

If these books are not available at your local newsstands and if you wish a free catalog of books, send price indicated plus 10¢ per book to cover mailing costs to LANCER BOOKS, INC., 185 Madison Avenue, New York 16, N. Y.